DEATH'S MARK

BLOOD AND IRON SERIES
BOOK 1

NICK EFSTATHIOU
RON RIPLEY

EDITED BY SCARE STREET

CHAPTER 1
MASON

"This is wrong, James, and you know it," Kenny snapped.

James Thurber looked at the large man across the desk from him and crushed the fear that threatened to rise within him. The fact Kenny was angrily jabbing his thick index finger at him didn't help.

"I know how you feel, Kenny, I do," James replied.

Kenny raised a bushy eyebrow.

"Really, I do," James continued. "However, Mr. Pettigrew has established the fact that there are quotas which this factory needs to fill. Quotas, mind you, which will put money in your pocket."

"I don't deny that I'll be making money," Kenny grumbled. "The issue is that it won't be at overtime rates. And, according to the letter we got yesterday, we're losing our dental benefits."

"The dental is just until Mr. Pettigrew can find us a better deal," James smiled. "And just think, that dental insurance money is going back into your paycheck."

Kenny's expression darkened. "Back where it's going to be taxed, and it's not enough to cover the cost of a dental examine."

James shook his head. "I'm sorry, Kenny. This is totally out of my hands."

"I know that. We all know that," Kenny said. "What you don't know is us. You're not from here, James. You didn't work your way up from the factory floor. You're Mr. Pettigrew's man, and you're doing his work. Well, we'll do his work, too, but we're not going to be killing ourselves over it. Best to make sure he's built in some leeway in those quotas of his."

James stiffened. "Are you threatening the factory?"

Kenny's eyes widened with mock innocence. "What? Not at all. I'm just telling you to remind Mr. Pettigrew that we're human beings, after all. Working extra hours with no incentive tends to bring down morale and causes a lag in production. I'm sure you learned that in college. It must be covered in one business class or another. Well, I'll see you Monday."

"There's a shift for Saturday," James said, his voice harsh. "You're on it."

Kenny looked at James. "I don't think so, James. I haven't worked a Saturday shift in as long as I can remember. I'm not about to change that now."

James watched with growing fury as Kenny exited the office, closing the door behind him. He listened as the man's heavy boots thundered down the stairs that led to the warehouse, knowing full well Kenny would cut through the warehouse to the factory floor.

He would cut through and tell everyone he saw how unreasonable James and Mr. Pettigrew were.

Kenny would tell them he wasn't working the Saturday shift.

Mr. Pettigrew had not built in any leeway for the delivery of his quotas. And why should he? It's not like jobs were easy to come by up in Mason, New Hampshire. When Mr. Pettigrew purchased the factory, he had been assured by the previous owners that the workforce was dedicated and loyal to the company.

Evidently, that loyalty didn't remain if some of the rules were changed.

With his frown deepening, James picked up the phone.

Ezra Pettigrew hung up the phone and allowed himself a deep, angry frown.

For several minutes, the expression remained on his face, and then he relaxed his features, forcing himself to calm down.

Decisions made in anger were rarely well-thought-out or profitable.

Ezra never made an angry decision. It went against making money, which was the only thing in life he enjoyed.

Recalcitrant employees were nothing new to him. He had purchased factories in economically depressed areas around the country, and they all turned a tidy profit in the end. It was getting the workers to that point, however, which usually proved difficult.

New Hampshire would be no exception.

But there was one difference. Ezra could no longer use the "muscle" he had employed in the past. In Illinois, he had hired some rather unsavory characters to encourage his workers to go the extra mile, as it were. Rather than seeing an increase in work performance, Ezra had been shocked to learn that three men had been beaten to death, and a fourth was in a coma. All in an effort to return his employees to the factory.

The brutal deaths of the men hadn't bothered Ezra quite as much as the very real possibility of someone following the money back to him and linking him to the violence. He hated the physical act of beating someone, which was why he paid good money to ensure it was done properly and efficiently.

The mistakes in Illinois had soured him on the whole idea of hiring goons for assistance. Yet, without some way to threaten unwilling workers, Ezra wouldn't turn a profit.

And not making money was unacceptable.

He had, fortunately, found a possible alternate solution, although it would require him to spend time in Mason, New Hampshire, which wasn't a place he wanted to be.

Still, the desire for money was there.

Ezra reached out, picked up his desk phone and dialed his assistant.

"Sir?" Robert asked.

"Could you book me the soonest flight to New Hampshire? I'll also need accommodations for three weeks in a reputable hotel within a half-hour commute, perhaps a little longer, to my facility in Mason," Ezra stated.

"Will you be dining in or out, sir?" Robert asked, and Ezra could hear the man's pen scratching across the surface of a notepad.

"Dining out, please, Robert," Ezra answered.

"And shall I have Abigail pack for you?"

Ezra chuckled. "Please, Robert. Thank you very much."

"Of course, sir. I'll inform you as soon as I have the itinerary prepared."

"Excellent." Ezra ended the call and then picked up his cell phone. He dialed a number jotted down on a scrap of paper, and when he heard someone answer, he said, "Methuselah."

There was a soft click, and a different, older voice spoke. "With whom am I speaking?"

"My name is Ezra Pettigrew," Ezra stated. "I have heard you sell haunted items."

"I offer curiosities of a specific sort to clients who specialize in oddities," the man remarked. "If you ask, I may well have it."

Ezra smiled. "I'm looking for something small. Something discreet."

The older man chuckled. "Sir, I can assure you that everything I have is discreet."

CHAPTER 2
THE HIGHWAY OF DEATH

Stan Owens sat in the front sitting room of Marilyn's boarding house, looking out the window and finishing the last of his tea. Despite it being past seven in the morning, the other tenants of the house were quiet. Most, if not all, had stayed out late at the few bars in the area, while a handful, such as Adam Henderson, merely enjoyed the extra time to sleep. The young man was, as Marilyn often stated, worth his weight in gold around the house.

Stan agreed.

Setting his empty teacup down on its saucer, Stan took his reading glasses out of his vest pocket, placed them upon the bridge of his nose and removed his small notebook from his suit coat's inner pocket. Despite knowing exactly what was scheduled for the day, he took comfort in reviewing it.

At eight o'clock, Kenny Langsam would arrive. Kenny was never late, nor was he early. He arrived precisely at the agreed upon time.

The two of them would, the schedule stated, speak from eight to ten. They did so every Saturday and had done so since Stan had first gone to the VFW after his return home from Iraq and his discharge from the Army.

Stan swallowed dryly at the memory, put the notebook away and returned his glasses to his vest pocket. As he regained his composure, the whisper of Marilyn's feet on the sitting room's polished wooden floor caught his attention. He turned in time to see her approaching from the right, a fresh cup of tea in hand.

"How are you, Stan?" she asked, taking his empty cup and replacing it with the fresh arrival.

"The same as always, I'm afraid," he remarked.

She nodded. Marilyn understood. Her husband had succumbed to nightmares of war that hadn't left him alone.

"Did you remember tonight is bridge night?" she asked.

Stan hesitated, then replied, "No. I had forgotten. I'm certain it is in my notebook."

"I am as well," Marily agreed with a small smile. "I watched you write it down. I'm afraid Loreen will be here this evening."

Stan attempted to repress a wince and failed. Loreen's voice struck with the force of a blow, and Stan clenched his teeth at the mere thought of it.

"I will, of course, find another place to stay until the game is finished," Stan told her.

"Perhaps you could go out with Adam. He tends to visit Dow's Bar and Grille on Saturdays."

Stan nodded. "That is an excellent suggestion. It has been some time since I went to Dow's."

Marilyn smiled, turned and left the room as quietly as she had entered it. Stan shifted his attention back to the windows and kept himself occupied with examining the world beyond. It was far better to catalog the details of the nearest elm than it was to remember too much.

A short time later, as the mantel clock struck eight, the back door opened, and Kenny's familiar, heavy footsteps sang out on the kitchen's linoleum floor. Stan heard the man's gruff voice greet Marilyn, knew from memory that she would demand a quick hug from the towering man, and then the footsteps continued.

Within a moment, Kenny entered the room, his head barely clearing the top of the doorframe. Stan went to rise from his seat, as he always did, and following the same script, Kenny chuckled and motioned for Stan to remain where he was.

The chair opposite Stan's groaned as Kenny lowered himself into it, a broad smile playing across the older man's face.

"How are you, Stan?" Kenny asked.

"I am tolerable," Stan replied. "How are you?"

"Likewise," Kenny sighed. Marilyn entered the room and handed Kenny a large ceramic mug of steaming black coffee. "Thank you, Marilyn. You're the best."

Stan caught a glimpse of a blush on Marilyn's face, and not for the first time, he wondered if there had ever been anything between the two of them.

Marilyn exited and Kenny held the mug in both hands, the steam rising to curl around his broad features and highlight the etched decades of laughter and worry around his eyes.

"You look like you had a rough night," Kenny observed after a moment.

"I did."

"Nightmares?"

"Yes," Stan nodded.

"Thought any more about talking to one of the docs at the VA in Manchester?"

"I am not particularly fond of the Veterans Administration," Stan answered, his tone sharper than he intended it to be.

Kenny smiled at him. In a gentler voice, the man said, "I know you're not. Not many of us are. But there are good people there, and the VA in Manchester has some solid people. I'm going to ask you every week, you know that."

Stan sighed. "Yes."

"Good," Kenny grinned. He took a drink from his coffee. "Damn, that woman knows how to brew a cup of coffee."

"It seems to me," Stan observed, "that there is very little that Marilyn does not know how to do."

"You're right about that," Kenny agreed. "Well, it's my turn to lead off, right?"

"Yes."

"So, work's been a damned nightmare," Kenny stated. "Got a new owner. He's already cutting benefits and demanding overtime work without compensation."

Stan raised an eyebrow.

"Oh, no, it's not going to stand," Kenny told him. "We'll get our pay, but it might be painful for a bit. Other than work, everything's been good."

"Even at home?" Stan asked.

"Especially at home," Kenny said. "At times, it's too quiet now that Buster's passed. He was a good dog, and I miss the hell out of him, but he was old. Real old. And he's buried right out back by the birch trees. Oh, that reminds me, the Adirondack chair came in this week. It's all prepped and ready. I put it out by Buster's grave, and I've got that fire pit too. May not be able to have the dog sit next to me, but I sure as hell can sit by him."

Stan nodded in understanding. His own dog had died when he was in the Army, and he'd not had another in over thirty years.

"Were the nightmares any different?" Kenny asked.

"Yes," Stan admitted, and Kenny looked at him with surprise.

"Really?"

"Yes." Stan turned his attention to his shoes for a moment, then back to his friend. "I was back in Iraq. Back on the highway."

Kenny sipped his coffee and listened.

Stan sighed. "While I have dreamed of it before, last night was different. For some reason, last night, I could smell it."

"Smell what?"

"Death," Stan told him. "I could smell the burnt corpses and the burning rubber. The diesel fumes and the strange tang of overheated metal. I could even smell the desert."

A silence fell over them as Stan discovered he couldn't speak. His throat had tightened, and his body had gone stiff.

"Were you sweating when you woke up?" Kenny asked.

"Yes," Stan whispered. "A cold sweat."

"Did you wake up before the attack?"

Stan nodded. "Right before. I was walking up to the truck. It had a body in the driver's seat. He was fused to the metal frame, and I remember seeing his teeth. Gold. He had gold fillings and gold-framed glasses. They were melted to the bridge of his nose and the side of his head. I was reaching for him. I do not even know why. The reason for it escapes me, no matter how hard I think about it."

"Don't think too hard about it, Stan," Kenny told him. "There are some things we do that there's really no explanation for. This is just one of them."

Stan took a sip of his tea. "It was, I confess, a difficult night for me."

"Sounds like it. What do you have planned for the rest of the day?"

"I will do some work around the house for Marilyn," Stan replied. "There is still much to do to prepare it for winter. After that, I hope to accompany Adam to Dow's."

Kenny let out a surprised laugh. "That a fact?"

Stan offered him a small smile. "It is surprising, I know. It has been some time since I went out for a drink. In fact, I cannot remember the last time I had a glass of beer."

"I do."

"You do?" Stan asked, surprised.

"Three years ago, at least," Kenny chuckled. "You were at Mayweather's retirement party. At Dow's, by the way. Mayweather offered you a beer, and you actually drank it."

Stan shook his head. "Alcohol and I no longer agree with each other. A quick hello now and again is acceptable, but no more."

"Bad time?"

"Nothing I wish to discuss," Stan answered, and his words were harsher than he meant. "My apologies, Kenny."

"No need, Stan. You know that. There's a reason I have my 20-year sobriety chip," Kenny continued. "Alcohol and I were too close to one another for a long time. My marriage was rough without whiskey. Unbearable with it. I'm just glad we didn't have kids."

Stan could hear the lies in his friend's voice, but he did not draw attention to it. There was no reason to linger on the mistakes of the past.

Kenny cleared his throat. "So, you're going out with Adam tonight?"

"I am," Stan nodded.

"And you're working around here for the day?"

Again, Stan confirmed with a nod.

"Okay, I've got a task for you, then."

Stan sipped his tea and waited.

"Go on down to the library today," Kenny told him. "They've got a new copy of a book by a Buddhist monk named Thich Nhat Hanh. It's about walking meditation. I want you to borrow it and read it by next Saturday, okay?"

Stan took his notebook out from his inner pocket and jotted the information down. "Yes, I will read this book by next Saturday. Is there anything else?"

"No," Kenny smiled. "Other than try and have fun tonight, okay?"

"I will try," Stan told his friend and finished his tea.

The men were tired, and the day had only just begun.

Jake Merchant looked at Mike Sullivan, and the two men shook their heads. The job was worse than their boss had let on, but that didn't surprise them. He was always giving them the worst places to pick up.

Sometimes, it worked out, like when Mike salvaged a box of 1940s baseball cards. They'd pawned that in Concord and drank for four days straight. Or when Jake had managed to find a wallet that still had money in it, even though the driver's license had expired in '52.

But those times were few and far between.

Not only had the boss sent them on a bad job, but it was in Mason, out in the middle of nowhere.

"Dude," Mike moaned. "This is it. We're not going to get that other bay in here. We've got to go dump it."

Jake nodded and looked back into the now-empty bay of the three-car garage. The building had sunk to the left and leaned precariously forward. Rot had settled into the dull gray wood, and moss grew on the ancient shingles covering the roof. Not a single window remained unbroken, and Jake wondered how long it had stood this way.

"We ought to be able to fit that trunk on," Jake said, pointing at a small suitcase. The dark green piece of luggage stood at the far end of the cleared-out bay.

"You want to crack it open first?" Mike asked.

Jake shook his head. "Nah. Toss it up in the back, and we can pick through it up at the landfill. I want to grab a cup of coffee. My head's killing me."

Mike gave him a thumbs-up, went back into the garage and retrieved the luggage. As Mike tossed it up and over the edge of the small truck, Jake climbed into the driver's seat and started the engine. A moment later, Mike got into the passenger's seat, and the two men took out their cigarettes. They each lit a Newport, exhaled, and then Mike shifted the truck into gear.

The truck rumbled out over the rutted, hard-packed dirt of the driveway, and he turned hard onto the street, the tires groaning as they climbed up over the broken asphalt.

Within a few minutes, he eased the truck into town, well aware of how the local cops liked messing with the trucks. He didn't want to get pulled over, especially since his license was expired and he had two DUIs on it.

He swore as a cat darted out in front of the truck, and he slammed on the brakes.

The tires squealed, and the cat vanished into the bushes across the street.

Jake muttered under his breath, turned the wheel hard and saw something fall out of the back and crash onto the pavement. For a moment, he considered going back for it, but when he saw it was the green piece of luggage, and the thing had snapped open, he didn't bother.

The luggage had lain on its side and Jake had seen it was empty.

There was no reason to pick the suitcase up at all.

* * *

Ian Sampson hated the 6th grade and everything to do with school. Especially since he had a report due on Monday and his mother had found out. Now, on Saturday morning, he had to walk to the library to do research that he could have done at home, on his iPad, after his soccer games.

But his mother had said he needed to learn a lesson, and apparently, that lesson was you aren't allowed to have fun if you forget a project.

Ian hated the library. Always did. Don't talk, be nice, don't run.

He rolled his eyes at the memories of all the reprimands he'd received at the school library and the Mason Library. And the worst part was, he couldn't mess around. Not today. If he got thrown out, he wouldn't be able to finish the project.

If he didn't finish the project, mom was pulling him off the soccer team and locking the gaming systems up until 7th grade.

Ian knew she would. His mom always "followed through" when it came to anything. Grandma said it was great, but he didn't agree. Not one bit.

Ahead of him, Ian saw something strange, a sort of suitcase on the pavement. He kept his eyes on it as he walked, and then he remembered a story from school about kids finding money in a suitcase left in the woods. His mom had said it was an urban legend, whatever that was, but Ian knew it was true. Andy Short had been one of the kids to find it, and he always had money with him.

When Ian reached the suitcase, he checked both ways and then stepped off the sidewalk to grab the handle. He picked it up, hurried back and moved a few feet into the woods. Poking through the suitcase, he found three old coin bags. The first one he opened had $72 in it, and his heart started to race.

The second one had another $29.

Ian stuffed all the money into his front pocket before he lifted the third, which was heavier than the first two, and it didn't jingle.

Ian's heart thumped against his chest, and a shiver of excitement raced up his spine. He struggled with the clasp, and then, with a snap, it popped open as it tumbled from his hands onto the ground. Thick rock salt, like what his mother put down on the driveway in the winter, spilled out. A thin sliver of silver stood out from the salt, and Ian reached for it.

His fingertips brushed aside the salt, and when his skin touched the silver, he howled with pain. As he jerked his hand back, the movement caused the silver to fall out onto a battered leaf.

Ian shook his hand, expecting to see blood on his fingertips.

But there was nothing.

He looked at the silver item and saw it was a small, decorative letter L. Something flickered a few feet away, and Ian glanced at it.

He blinked, shook his head, and got to his feet, unsure of where the woman had come from.

She was old, and she wore clothes that didn't look like clothes. Her face was haggard, and he wasn't sure if it was real or makeup like the haunted houses with actors paid to do jump scares.

She shifted her feet, and when she did, Ian realized he could see through her. He could see everything through her.

The woman bent over, grunted and picked up the silver L. It started to sink through her hand, but she caught it with the other. Her body shimmered, almost as though it were hardening.

She looked up at him and frowned. "Who are you, boy?"

"Ian," he whispered, unable to stop himself from answering.

"I'm Lotta," she mumbled. "Where am I?"

"Mason, New Hampshire."

Lotta nodded. "Sheriff's still where he used to be? Downtown, 'cross from city hall?"

"Yes ma'am," he whispered, shivering.

"Good." She glanced around. "Where you headed?"

"Library. Project."

Lotta nodded. "Good. If my boy'd done that, he mightn't have been shot by the sheriff. Still, ain't no cause to kill'm. I wouldn't have died alone if they hadn't a shot'm."

"I'm sorry," Ian whispered.

"Ain't no, never mind," Lotta snorted. "Get on to the library, Ian."

Ian stumbled his way out of the woods and onto the sidewalk, where he turned and looked back.

Lotta flashed him a smile of yellowed and crooked teeth and faded, the silver L falling to earth with a strangely sickening thud.

Ian ran for the library.

CHAPTER 4
ACCEPTABLE ACCOMMODATIONS

Ezra sat at the desk in the suite of rooms Robert had found for him. All his necessities, as well as a variety of clothing, had been packed by Abigail and were neatly put away. As much as Ezra missed the unique skill sets brought by his two personal assistants, he had no desire to place them in the mix of what he was planning on doing. They were loyal, and loyalty must always be rewarded.

Ezra looked at his written list. He tapped his pen against the knuckles of his right hand and then jotted down one last thought in his own shorthand.

Kenny must go first.

Ezra had no doubt that a cryptologist of any worth would be able to crack his shorthand, should that cryptologist also be fluent in the Latin of Julius Caesar.

Ezra allowed himself a short chuckle at the thought of someone attempting to decipher his handwriting, then his shorthand, and finally, the style in which Julius Caesar had written his *Commentary on the Gallic Wars*. It was a small sense of smugness Ezra enjoyed. He wondered if Brother Ralph of the Brothers of the Sacred Heart would have appreciated the way Ezra employed the Latin the brother had so diligently drilled into their heads.

Ezra hoped the man was burning in Hell and lamenting all of his poor life choices.

Shaking away the memories of old abuse, Ezra focused once more on the current situation. The factory was in Mason, New Hampshire. The workers who refused to accept change.

With a dissatisfied sigh, Ezra stood and walked into the main room. Placed in the middle of a large table was a small, ornate wooden box. The interior, he knew, was lined with lead, and a single button from an old Navy peacoat lay within.

Ezra walked around the table, inspecting the line of salt he had placed earlier in the morning. He had no desire to be taken unawares by a ghost of any sort, let alone one he was going to employ for violence.

Assured that all was in order, Ezra reached out to the box, flipped up its lid and stepped back. He waited a moment, then shrugged and retreated to a chair. Humming to himself, he picked up a copy of *Treasure Island* he had brought with him and began to read.

He made it through twenty-one pages before the ghost appeared. Ezra did not acknowledge the dead man's presence and continued his reading. He knew the ghost would have been informed as to the situation, that the dead man would be sold. Some ghosts cared, others did not. All Ezra was concerned with, however, was whether the dead man would do as he was told.

Or asked, rather.

Asked, Ezra knew, was always better, although not nearly as much fun as ordering.

"Hello," the dead man said after Ezra had read several more pages.

Marking his place in the book with a finger, Ezra looked up at the dead man and smiled. The ghost hadn't died well. While Ezra had no history of the dead man's passing, it was clear that part of it was from a fire. Half of the ghost's face was a charred mass of flesh. He wore a Navy peacoat with insignia on it, but Ezra knew nothing of the Navy or its ranks. Like his face, half of the man's coat and his jeans were burned away, revealing the wounds on his body. One foot was clad in a short boot, the other was missing entirely, burned away.

No, the dead man hadn't died well at all.

"Hello," Ezra replied and introduced himself.

The dead man nodded. "I'm Theo."

"A pleasure," Ezra smiled and set his book down. "Were you informed as to why I purchased you?"

"Yeah, they said you needed a little muscle," Theo answered. "Not quite sure how I can help with that. What with me being dead and all."

"You would be surprised at what you can accomplish," Ezra told him. "Do you have a history of violence?"

"Well, I fought a hell of a lot," Theo answered. "Used to box on the USS *Intrepid*, too."

"Did you die while fighting?"

Theo shook his head. "No. I was getting ready for duty when a fire broke out. I don't remember much about it, I'm sorry to say. One minute, I'm trying to get a fire hose, next, I'm watching them commit my body to the deep."

Ezra frowned in confusion.

The dead man smiled. "Burial at sea."

"Ah," Ezra nodded. "Well, that makes perfect sense."

"You mentioned violence," Theo said, bringing the conversation back to the subject at hand, and Ezra appreciated the ghost's focus.

"I did. I need an individual capable of committing violence against a living person," Ezra explained. "I know there is no benefit to you, none that I can offer. You are dead, and being dead means you cannot enjoy the pleasures of the living."

"That's a fact." Theo's expression mirrored the glum tone he spoke with.

"However," Ezra continued, "I have heard of something rather strange. It seems that if a ghost were to inhabit a living person's flesh, they can enjoy those fleeting physical pleasures."

"Are you serious right now?" Theo asked.

"Quite," Ezra nodded. "I never make jokes when crafting a deal, Theo. It's bad for business. Now, from what I've read, the ghost must find a person under the influence of either alcohol or a narcotic. Once they do so, the ghost can then enjoy sensations such as touch, taste, and smell. All the senses, actually. Unfortunately, this lasts only until the mind-altering substance wears off. And you can never be quite certain of the person the ghost is going to be able to get into, if they can get into a person at all."

"What are you offering?" Theo asked.

"Just this," Ezra explained. "If you work for me and do as I ask, I will supply to you an individual of your choice, male or female, age doesn't matter. With the person obtained, I will be certain to put them into the necessary state of mind for you to take over and then provide you with whatever you wish. Alcohol, food, et cetera, et cetera."

Theo grinned, nodded and declared, "That sounds like a hell of a deal."

"I like to think it is," Ezra smiled. "Now, I'd offer to shake on it, but I think I'd come out the worse for the experience."

Theo chuckled. "That's for sure."

"Do we have the proverbial gentlemen's agreement, then?" Ezra asked.

"We do." Theo glanced around. "So, who do you need hurt?"

Kenny looked around the room and nodded with satisfaction. Two leaders from each shift had made it to the meeting, which made seven altogether.

Seven was a good and lucky number.

They sat in his den, cups of coffee in hand and the noonday sun streaming in through windows he had washed earlier in the morning.

"What's it going to be?" Annie Hamm asked.

"A vote on whether we slow down or keep at the pace this new guy Pettigrew wants," Kenny told her.

A soft grumble went through the room. Kenny knew how they all would vote. They weren't a union shop. Hadn't ever wanted to be one, and they still didn't. All they wanted was a little bit of fair play from Pettigrew and his dancing bear, James.

"Does anyone think this won't work?" Kenny asked.

They shook their heads in unison.

"Good," Kenny stated. "You know it's going to get hard before we get what we want, right?"

Mutters of acknowledgment filled the room.

"We're not going to get violent, right, Kenny?" Omer L'Étrange asked.

"Right," Kenny assured them. "Listen, guys. Violence won't do anything but cost us our jobs and land us in jail. Nobody wants that. Well, at least I don't."

The men and women in the room chuckled.

"What we'll do is slow down. Not enough to stop the lines, and sure as hell not enough to cost us our jobs. But we won't meet this extra damned quota Pettigrew has put in place." Kenny looked at them all. "He wants to pay us overtime, well, that's a different story. Until he does, though, we work our hours, and we don't put anything extra out. We've all got to be in agreement with this, or it just won't work. Anyone you can think of on your lines that won't get in line with the rest of us?"

"There's Janet Barker," Annie said after a moment. "She's got that sister of hers living with her. Plus, her nieces. Money's tight."

Kenny nodded, jotting down Janet's name. "If you talk to her, tell her I'll cover the difference. It's a gift, not a loan. Mind you, tell her that, too. Anybody other than Janet?"

Curtis La France cleared his throat. "We've got a few on third who might prove to be an issue. Young fellas come down from Vermont. They've no reason to join with a slow down."

"Have them come 'round to me," Kenny told Curtis. "I won't threaten or chase them out of the job or anything. But I'll see if we can't come to some sort of an agreement. That it?"

The men and women nodded.

"Right," Kenny smiled. "Let's drink our coffee and plan this out. We'd best be ready if they come in hard."

"Think they'll bring in the police?" Annie asked.

Kenny shook his head. "No. Worst thing for them to do. Pettigrew might bring in some muscle, but that wouldn't surprise me. If he does, well, we'll be ready for that, too."

Lifting his coffee mug up, Kenny looked around the room and declared, "Here's to getting paid what we're worth."

His coworkers echoed his toast, and the day marched on.

CHAPTER 5

EMILY'S UNCLE

Stan glanced at his watch.

It was half past two in the afternoon as he stood on the porch of Emily Yellen's home.

The younger woman opened the door a moment later and flashed a nervous smile at him, tucking a long lock of dyed blue hair behind her left ear.

"Mr. Owens," she greeted and stepped back, holding the door open for him.

"Please, Emily, call me Stan," he stated, moving into the hallway.

"Okay, Stan," she said, smiling tiredly. "I'm sorry. It's been a long week."

"And I am sorry for that. I wish you had called for me sooner."

"I would have, but my Aunt May thought it would take care of itself." Emily led the way into the kitchen, where she offered him a chair to sit on.

"It didn't take care of itself," Stan said.

"No," Emily sighed. "It surely didn't. Can I get you anything?"

"No, thank you, though," Stan replied, and the young woman sat down across from him at the battered kitchen table. "Is your aunt here?"

Emily shook her head. "She went back to Hollis this morning. Said she couldn't stand to be in the house anymore."

"I am surprised she spent more than an hour in here," Stan remarked. "Considering how poorly she and her husband got along."

Emily rolled her eyes. "Tell me about it. I always wondered why they didn't just get divorced."

"It was not in their makeup to do so," Stan said gently, and Emily nodded. "Has he told you yet where his item is?"

Anger flashed across the young woman's face. "No. And he said he won't, either. This morning, just before you came, he was screaming about how the house should have been his and not my mom's."

"Ah." Stan thought for a moment and then asked, "Emily, would you trust me to be alone in your home?"

"Of course," she answered without any hesitation.

"Thank you for your trust."

She smiled in response.

"I think if you remove yourself from the home for an hour, everything will be better when you return," Stan informed her.

"Really?" Emily's left eyebrow rose into an arc.

"Really," Stan answered, getting to his feet. "I will have a conversation with your uncle, and we will get the situation sorted for you."

"Thank you," Emily whispered. Then, in a louder voice, she added, "There's a bag of tea and a coffee cup by the stove. I put water in the kettle if you want to make yourself a cup."

"Thank you, Emily," Stan smiled.

She nodded and stood up, and Stan watched as she gathered her wallet and keys from the table. The younger woman smiled once more, then left by the side entrance.

He heard her car start, then back out of the driveway.

Stan was alone in the house with the dead.

"Paul," Stan called. "It's just the two of us now if you would care to speak with me."

Something rattled, then fell in one of the rooms off the main hallway.

Stan sat down again at the table. He would not chase after the dead man. Paul would, he knew, come to him sooner rather than later.

It was Paul's nature when the man was alive, and Stan had no doubt it would be the same with him dead.

And Stan was right.

Paul entered the kitchen and sat down in the chair recently occupied by Emily. The dead man did not look well, and Stan wasn't surprised by that, either. Paul had died from prostate cancer after refusing treatment and practicing a "whole health diet" that consisted only of barely cooked meats and moonshine.

"Why are you in my house, Stan?" Paul demanded.

"Paul," Stan began, "this is not your home."

"It is. This should have been mine, and everyone knows it," Paul grumbled, folding his arms over his chest. "It should have been mine, and now it is. No more trouble. Well, just a little bit. Emily needs to get out. May understood. She got out. About damned time, too."

"Emily is not leaving this house," Stan stated. "It was given to her by your parents. Your parents were quite adamant about you not receiving the home."

Paul swore at him.

Stan shrugged. "It does not matter what you say, Paul, the fact of the matter remains that this isn't your home."

"You need to leave."

"No," Stan replied, shaking his head. "I have no intention of exiting this place until you leave, too."

Paul chuckled. "I can make you go."

"No, you cannot."

Paul stood up and walked around the table to stand in front of Stan.

"Stan," Paul stated. "This is gonna hurt like hell."

"It might," Stan shrugged.

With a harsh laugh, the dead man reached out and put his hands on Stan. A look of pained surprise raced across the dead man's face, and he vanished, leaving nothing more than an uncomfortable tingling sensation on Stan's shoulders.

Getting to his feet, Stan walked to the stove, picked up the tea kettle and added water to it. From behind him, he heard Paul swear and then felt the dead man's hands on his back.

But the sensation was fleeting, chased by another growled curse from the ghost.

Paul tried to touch him twice more before Stan sat down at the table, the burner under the kettle beginning the slow progress of warming the water for tea.

Paul entered the room once more, keeping a wide distance between himself and Stan.

"Why can't I touch you?" Paul snapped.

Stan smiled. "For reasons I'd rather not discuss. Let us suffice to say that I am untouchable by the dead."

"I can find another way to force you out," Paul stated.

"Possibly," Stan acknowledged. "However, I am certain I can bring in someone who will find your object. If I am forced to do that, Paul, I will search for a way to destroy it."

"So?" Paul scoffed. "What's that going to do?"

"From what I have been able to ascertain, it would stop you from being able to haunt anywhere, let alone your niece's home."

"My home!" Paul snarled. He grabbed the table, and for a moment, it shook beneath his hands before he lost the ability to hold it. The dead man appeared startled.

"Tell me, Paul," Stan began, his voice soft. "Do you believe in an afterlife?"

The dead man snorted. "I'm proof that there is."

"No, not this," Stan continued in the same, low tone. "This can't be considered an afterlife. There are not enough ghosts."

Paul opened his mouth, then closed it.

Stan nodded. "You see the truth in my statement. If there are not enough ghosts here, that means they should be somewhere else. Or, perhaps there is more than one place. If I recall correctly, Paul, you and your people are Baptists, are you not?"

The dead man remained silent, but his eyes widened.

"I do not believe you made any sort of peace before you died," Stan told the ghost. "In fact, I imagine you were quite surprised when you awakened here, in this place, and not in either Heaven or Hell."

"Be quiet," Paul whispered.

Stan ignored him. "If I might make a further supposition, Paul, I do believe you were shocked not to awaken in Hell. Everyone except for your wife was aware of your amorous adventures on your business trips in Quebec. Do you believe those engagements were in keeping with the Bible?"

"Where am I going to go?" Paul hissed. "This is my home!"

"It was the home you were raised in, the home given to your niece by your parents. It is not your home, Paul. As for where you might go, I believe we can find some sort of place for you," Stan assured him.

The ghost licked his lips, a nervous habit carried from life into death. After a moment, the dead man whispered, "Are you sure?"

Stan nodded. "I am quite sure. What is your haunted item, Paul?"

"It's," Paul hesitated. "I had a toy car when I was a kid. My Uncle Ed gave it to me right before he died."

"Where is it?"

"In the pantry," Paul muttered. "There's a loose floorboard at the back. I used to hide stuff there because I knew my mom would search my room. She hated my Uncle Ed. If she knew he gave me something, she made it disappear when I was at school."

The kettle whistled, and Stan went to the stove. He turned off the heat, poured the water over the tea bag in the cup, and then returned the kettle to the burner. As the tea steeped, Stan shifted his attention to the pantry. Paul, he saw, sat at the table, anger on his face as he stared at the wall.

Stan opened the pantry, squatted down and removed several cans of soup, setting them aside on the floor. Cold air washed over him, and when Stan glanced to his left, he saw Paul squatting beside him.

"I'd forgotten it was here," Paul said, his tone gentle. "I'd even forgotten about Uncle Ed. But when I died, I woke up here. Not in Hell or Heaven. Not at the hospital or at home. Here, right in front of the pantry. Emily was at the stove, and she couldn't see me. I looked at the pantry, and I remembered. I remembered it all."

Stan reached into the back of the pantry, pressed down and felt the last board move. He slipped his free hand under the lip and extracted the board.

"It's on the right," Paul told him.

Stan's fingers moved around the right side of the small cavity, and then they brushed across a cold piece of metal. He closed his fingers around it and brought the toy car out into the open.

He found in his hand a battered, light blue Matchbox car.

"That's a Rolls Royce Silver Cloud," Paul whispered. "I used to wonder what it would be like to ride in a car like that. I didn't think I ever would, and I never did, but it was a great car to play with. My mom never saw it. Not once. I even hid it in my briefs one time when she barged in while I was getting dressed after a bath."

Stan remained silent.

"What will happen to it?" Paul asked.

"I have a special container I brought with me, Paul," Stan explained. "I will put your car in the box, and you will be in the box as well. I will bring you to my home and store you there, as I have stored some others. Someday, I hope, I will have a better plan, but for now, that is the best I can offer."

"It's better than Hell," Paul chuckled. He looked at Stan. "I've been a pain."

"You have."

The dead man laughed and shook his head. "You were irritating in life, Stan Owens, but that's because I didn't realize how much you did for the living and the dead. I apologize."

Surprised, Stan offered a weak smile before saying, "Thank you."

"Well, let's put me away before my bad attitude returns," Paul said, straightening up into a standing position.

Stan did the same and then reached into his suit coat's outer pocket. He removed a small, heavy box and slid the top open. The interior was lined with maroon velvet and was just large enough to fit the Matchbox car. As Stain placed the vehicle in it, he caught sight of Paul watching him.

"That velvet?" Paul asked.

"It is."

"I appreciate that," Paul told him. "Will I know what's going on?"

"I am not sure," Stan admitted. "I have not asked anyone that question."

"So, you definitely have more of these?"

"Oh yes," Stan nodded. "One or two more."

Before Paul could speak again, Stan slid the box lid closed, and the dead man vanished, sealed behind the lead lining hidden by the velvet.

Stan returned the box to his pocket and then went to the countertop. He retrieved his tea and brought the cup to the table. Before going to the refrigerator to see if Emily had stocked any cream, he stepped back over to the pantry and cleaned up his mess.

He had come to fix a problem, not cause another.

CHAPTER 6
WORKING FOR PAYDAY

Ezra stepped off the elevator, his package tucked under one arm while holding the door's passkey with the other. He had worked up a fine sweat in the hotel's gym and enjoyed an excellent massage afterward.

All he needed now was a good shower, something light to eat, and he could tackle the rest of the afternoon.

Ezra had woken up later than usual, which hadn't upset him as much as he thought it would. He had forgotten how good it felt to sleep in every once in a while. Making a habit of it would be bad, of that he had no doubt. But the occasional extra sleep was something the body needed, and he had to remember that.

Especially now when he was working, for all intents and purposes, alone. Robert and Abigail were hundreds of miles away, and for the first time in quite a while, he was on his own.

It was, he thought with a smile, exhilarating.

Ezra entered the suite of rooms, set the package down on the table and closed the door behind him. He walked to the desk, checked his phone for messages and saw there were only two, both from James.

Ezra sighed, placed the phone down and retreated to the bathroom, where he started the shower. Once he had the water adjusted to the proper temperature, he went about the business of getting his clothes ready. Soon, Ezra stood beneath the showerhead, eyes closed and enjoying the pulsating rhythm of the water. As the shower worked its wonders, Ezra heard the cell phone ring, and he rolled his eyes, hating the sound.

Despite his hatred of the phone, he knew it was essential. If he didn't have constant contact with his businesses, he wouldn't make money.

Still, he did appreciate the occasional bout of silence.

Ezra felt certain the call had been from James. The man was panicky about the business with the factory in Mason. Ezra lathered up, rinsed off, and quickly finished in the bathroom. He was buttoning his shirt as he reached the desk, and with a flick of his thumb, he brought up the call history on his phone.

James again.

Ezra cleared his throat, made sure he was in a calm and controlled place and called James back.

"Mr. Pettigrew," James started, the words tumbling out of his mouth.

"Slow down, James," Ezra said calmly. "Tell me what's going on."

"I think they're going to do it!" James blurted.

"Do what?"

"A slow down!"

Ezra frowned but maintained his composure. "Has there been any sort of evidence?"

"Two people from the Saturday shift called in sick. The two line leads," James responded.

"That is suspicious," Ezra agreed. "All right, here's what I want you to do. Are you listening?"

"Yes, sir."

"Good. Now, this is going to sound strange," Ezra continued. "But I want you to close your office for the day and go home."

"Am I being fired, sir?" James asked, his voice stiff.

"Not at all," Ezra assured him. "James, there are times when we must do what the workers do not expect. They believe that with a slowdown, you will be confused and irate, things you will most certainly pass on to me. But this isn't my first rodeo, as the saying goes. Not by a long shot. They won't expect you to go home. That is what I want you to do, though.

Go home and don't return until regular hours on Monday."

"And if there's a problem at the factory?" James asked.

"I'm hopeful there won't be," Ezra answered. "If there is, you'll have to respond as you normally would. But for now, don't give them anything. Be polite and be gracious, but don't offer any sort of explanation as to why you're leaving. Am I understood, James?"

"Yes, sir," the man replied, but Ezra heard the underlying confusion.

"You need to trust me, James. Do you?"

James coughed. "I do, sir. I do."

"Excellent. Go home, do something that helps you relax, and call me should anything happen to the factory while you're gone."

"I will, sir."

Ezra ended the call and brought the phone with him to the dining table. He didn't think James would call again, but should he, Ezra wanted to be able to reach it quickly. Any additional call would be a true emergency. Now that James had his marching orders, the man would carry them out.

Ezra turned his attention to the package on the table. It was small, the yellow outer wrap stained by rain, but the shipping label was well protected. He suspected the items inside were as well. The Methuselah shop prided itself on delivering its items safely, and Ezra appreciated the company's efforts to do so.

Ezra retrieved a pair of scissors from the desk, sat down again at the table and proceeded to open the package slowly. He took his time, concerned about damaging anything inside. When he finished, he had two boxes, one slightly larger than the other, standing on the table.

He considered waiting a bit before opening them but recalled the panicked notes in James' voice.

No, waiting was not an option at this time. Not with James being on edge nor with the current mood of the difficult factory workers.

Standing up, Ezra walked around the table, inspecting the line of salt. It was, he discovered, unbroken, and that brought a smile to his face. The line's continuity was a sure sign that it was the right time to work on the Mason issue.

Ezra reached for the boxes, flipped up the lids and retreated to the kitchen. He doubted the ghosts would be quick to make themselves known, and Ezra wanted another cup of coffee.

Humming *The Yellow Rose of Texas*, Ezra looked at the selection of K-Cups and waited for the dead to arrive.

Chapter 7
AT THE DINER

Stan sipped at his last cup of tea for the day, barring anything extraordinary occurring between dinner and bedtime. He adjusted himself on the bench seat and glanced out the diner window at Mason. A few vehicles rumbled past, and several people he knew stood a little further down the street in front of the Post Office.

"Hello, Stan," Ellen greeted as she came up to his booth. The younger woman smiled at him and didn't bother with getting out the order pad. "Adam called a minute ago."

Stan raised an eyebrow and waited, his hands wrapped around the cup of tea.

"Said he'll be along soon and to start without him," she smiled. "He's a nice fella."

Stan smiled back. "He is a good man, Ellen, and a fine friend. I enjoy his company."

She gave a happy nod and fidgeted with a simple leather bracelet she wore around her right wrist. "It's Saturday. Are you having your regular?"

"Mack made his meatloaf?" Stan asked, and Ellen laughed at the question.

"He makes it just for you, Stan, you know that."

"I wish he wouldn't do such a thing," Stan murmured.

"Stanley Owens," Ellen said, her voice carrying the faintest hint of a reprimand, "you need to learn how to accept thanks and accept it gracefully. That man would give the shirt off his back to you. Accept his offering of food, or you might shame him."

Stan's cheeks burned for a moment from the chastisement, and then, he nodded. "You are right, of course, Ellen. Thank you."

She leaned over the table, gave him a quick peck of a kiss on the top of his head and responded, "You're quite welcome, Stan. I'll tell Mack you're here. He'll get the food ready, and he'll start Adam's, too."

Stan nodded and drank a little more of his tea as she walked away.

The accepting of thanks was always difficult for him, especially when it occurred every day. Mack fed him, Marilyn housed him, and Sheriff Bowman would take him anywhere he wished. And they weren't the only ones.

Far from it.

At times, it seemed as though everyone in Mason would bend over backward for Stan, and he could never understand why.

The bell over the entrance to the diner chimed and interrupted his thoughts. A quick lookup showed Adam walking in, the man a far cry healthier and happier than he had been when Stan had first met him. Gone was the beaten, weathered look of a man struggling under the burden of homelessness and the scars of conflicts past.

Adam hid his struggles beneath a shine brought about by the joy of being part of a community. And the joy of working with Stan when it was called for.

Adam had showered and changed into a good pair of jeans, clean boots, and a black and gray checkered flannel shirt. His short black hair was combed back from his forehead, and he grinned with pure joy.

Adam slid into the seat across from Stan, asking, "How are you?"

"Tolerable," Stan replied, finishing his tea. "And you?"

"The same," Adam chuckled. "Did you get over to Emily Yellen's place?"

Stan nodded.

"Did you get her uncle?"

"I did."

"And did you put him away?" Adam asked, his voice filled with unrestrained curiosity.

"No, I did not," Stan replied. "Tomorrow, we will put him away. Plus, I need to show you how to make the boxes we require."

Adam's face paled. "I don't want to mess it up."

"You will not mess anything up, Adam," Stan assured him. "You are a smart young man. You will be fine. Trust me."

Adam cleared his throat, nodded, and forced a smile.

Ellen returned a short time later, placing a glass of water in front of Stan and a cup of coffee in front of Adam. The plate she set down beside Stan's water was piled high with mashed potatoes, corn, and several thick slices of meatloaf. The smell that wafted up from the dish made him salivate. As he picked up his flatware, Ellen chuckled and turned her attention to Adam.

"I'll have your steak out in a minute or two," she informed him.

Adam nodded his thanks and made himself comfortable.

From prior experience, Stan knew Adam didn't want him to wait, and so Stan didn't. He ate with precise movements, cutting one piece and eating it before moving on to the next.

"You eat like a machine," Adam stated, repeating an observation he had made in the past.

Stan paused. "I eat efficiently."

"Were you raised to eat like that?"

This was a new line of questioning, and it caused Stan to frown.

"No," he answered after a moment, considered adding more information, and then deciding not to.

Some memories he did not enjoy sharing.

Adam didn't press, and in a moment, seemed to have forgotten all about it.

Ellen delivered Adam's food, and soon, the men had finished their dinner. After Ellen cleared the dishes and poured another cup of coffee for Adam and one of water for Stan, Adam began to speak.

"Did Marilyn tell you I'm up at Mr. Thorpe's orchard?"

Stan nodded.

"There was something a little strange today," Adam continued, clearing his throat and taking a sip of his coffee.

Stan waited.

"Um, out at the back of the orchard, there's an old foundation. I guess there was an apple press in it before," Adam told him. "Mr. Thorpe said it was torn down when his brother died in it. Some of the machinery fell and crushed his brother's head."

"What did you see?" Stan asked.

"I thought I saw a kid," Adam's voice trembled. "I looked around, then went back to picking up the cuttings. But I kept seeing the kid out of the corner of my eye."

"Do you remember what the child looked like?" Stan asked.

"Yeah. Blue flannel shirt, jeans, pair of tennis shoes, and a mess of blood and bone where his head had been." Adam's hand shook as he lifted the coffee mug, some of the brew spilling out onto the table.

"Mr. Thorpe's brother," Stan said.

"I figured it was," Adam agreed. "I was wondering if maybe you'd want to go and check it out with me. I'm not sure what the boy wants, if anything."

"Yes, we can go whenever you wish."

Adam smiled with relief, took another drink of coffee and said, "I don't think I could do it alone, Stan."

"Well," Stan replied. "You don't have to."

A pleasant silence fell over the two men, and Stan glanced out the window to the street. On the sidewalk across from the diner, an older woman stood. She appeared confused and angry, and there was something familiar about her that tugged at Stan's memories.

"You okay?" Adam asked.

Stan shifted his attention back to Adam and nodded. "Yes. I saw someone who looked familiar."

Stan looked out the window again, but the woman was no longer in view. "Oh well, it appears she has moved on."

"Familiar in a good way or a bad way?" Adam asked with a grin.

"Not in any way you are imagining, Adam," Stan replied in a mildly rebuking tone.

Adam chuckled and returned his focus to his coffee.

Stan shook his head and wondered how he knew the woman.

CHAPTER 8
THEO

Ezra closed the two new boxes with a distinct sense of anger.

He had waited several hours for the new ghosts to show themselves, but they had not. It was, he knew, a difficult process at times, but it upset him, nonetheless.

And he disliked being upset.

He picked up his phone and sent a quick text to Robert.

I would prefer Indian this evening. Please have a car pick me up at six and make reservations for six thirty.

Robert's response came within two minutes.

Everything is prepared, sir.

Ezra smiled, and his anger decreased significantly. Assistants like Robert and Abigail were rare.

Ezra removed the two boxes from the table, placed them in the small kitchenette and returned Theo's container to the table. He opened the box and stepped away.

Theo appeared a moment later.

"Have you decided to send me out?" Theo asked.

"Almost," Ezra informed him. "I'm currently working out how best for you to interact with the individual."

Theo frowned. "I figured I'd just punch him a few times."

Ezra shook his head. "Unfortunately, that might leave some trace evidence."

"How in the hell could it do that?" Theo asked, confused.

"Too much contact between the dead and living flesh results in frostbite of varying degrees," Ezra explained. "This is why we have to limit the amount of contact made and why we need to have a plan in place before anything begins."

Theo grunted. "A plan I have to follow right through?"

"No," Ezra chuckled. "That wouldn't make any sense. I can't tell you to stick to a plan that is most likely going to change as soon as you make contact. No, the plan will serve as a framework. I want you to be able to know what needs to be done and then accomplish the task while staying within the framework of the final goal."

Theo frowned but didn't respond.

"Now," Ezra continued. "You said you were a fighter."

"Yup."

"Good. That means you're strong and quick."

Theo smiled. "Something like that."

"I think," Ezra said, "that I want the person to commit suicide."

Theo blinked, and the smile faded. "How the hell am I supposed to do that without touching him?"

"You're going to have to touch him at least once or twice," Ezra replied. "I don't know how much force you might need to knock someone out, but I believe you'll need to do that first."

"Okay," Theo muttered. "Let's say I knock this guy out. Great. I ain't got that much fine motor control anymore. How am I supposed to make it look like he killed himself?"

"Hmm." Ezra scratched his chin. "Yes, that's an aspect I hadn't thought of. I don't think he'll have a pistol. At least not one you'd be able to get at easily."

"Do you want me to work with a living person on this?"

"No," Ezra said quickly. "Not at all. A living person might talk, and that I cannot have. No, I need someone who won't talk."

"Most people don't even hear us," Theo sighed.

"Which brings us back to the problem of making a convincing-looking suicide scene." Ezra walked to a chair and sat down. "You were a sailor?"

Theo grinned. "Damned right I was."

"So, you know knots?"

"You're thinking of a hangman's knot?" Theo asked.

Ezra nodded.

"Sure, I could do one when I was alive. I'm not sure about now, I've never tried."

"Can you move things?" Ezra asked, leaning forward.

"Sometimes, if I'm focused enough."

"Good. Practice makes perfect," Ezra smiled. He glanced at his watch. It was quarter to six. "I'm going to get a tie and put it on the table. Could you practice and try to make a hangman's knot with it?"

Theo shrugged. "Sure, I can do it. You goin' out?"

"I am."

"You still goin' to hold up your end of the bargain?" Theo's voice was filled with doubt.

"Theo," Ezra answered, fixing a steady gaze on the dead man, "I am a businessman. I don't break deals. That's bad business. I will keep my end of the bargain. When all is said and done, you will have a body to use, a body to experience physical pleasure and sensation with once again."

"Okay," Theo nodded. "Get the tie, and I'll start working on it."

Ezra smiled and retrieved a simple black tie from his wardrobe. When he tossed it onto the table, both he and Theo grinned.

"This'll be fun," Theo admitted. "A challenge."

"Good. I look forward to seeing how you've done when I return."

Gathering up his wallet and passkey, Ezra hurried out of the suite. As the door clicked shut behind him, he thought of the dead man possibly succeeding, and that idea would make the forthcoming meal all the sweeter.

CHAPTER 9

HOME

Marilyn looked at him, and Stan stopped.

"Are you going for a walk?" she asked, and her question told him that not only did she know where he intended to go, but that she disapproved of it as well.

Stan appreciated her concern.

"I am," he confirmed.

She shook her head, then reached over to the umbrella stand by the door. Her long fingers picked out the walking stick he favored and handed it over. The stick was old, far older than Stan, and still had a fine, bright varnish upon it. Its length was punctuated by small knobs, and the tip was capped with a heavy bit of steel. In his hand, the smooth top of the stick felt perfect.

Stan did not need the stick to walk. His legs worked fine, as did his hips. No, the cane was something to hold onto when he reached his destination. Marilyn knew and disliked the place he was headed to, and at times Stan thought he might love her for it.

"Thank you, Marilyn."

She nodded. "You don't have to go there, Stan. You know this."

"I do," Stan agreed. "However, I must check on it with my own eyes."

"All right, then," she sighed. "I will see you when you return. Remember, Adam will be waiting for you."

Stan chuckled. "Yes, I will remember."

Marilyn opened the door for him, and he left the house, the steel tip of the stick thunking heavily upon the porch stairs and then the walkway itself.

He moved at a steady pace, walking neither too quickly nor dawdling. He nodded to several people he knew, smiled at others, and appreciated that no one attempted to interrupt his brief expedition.

His feet followed the streets of their own accord, turned where he needed to turn, and eventually brought him to the long, winding driveway. Stan came to a stop, standing at the border of the driveway and the road. He looked up the long and narrow drive to the dark house that sat atop the small rise. He did not bother to look at the mailbox to see if there was anything in it. All mail went to the post office, and from there to him.

Stan squatted down at the right side of the entrance, brushed away a bit of dirt and saw the gray PVC pipe was visible through a thick layer of Plexiglass. A dull green light glowed, and he felt a small bit of relief.

Standing up, Stan stepped onto the driveway.

Silence greeted him, and he walked through it. Around him, the thickening trees stretched to the sky, and the silence became heavier. Ahead of him, he saw the house, a grand structure in the Victorian style. Decorative gingerbread hung from the gables, and a variety of styles of shingles highlighted various aspects of the home.

For Mason, New Hampshire, the construction of the house had been a feat. Few people at the time of its construction had thought Mason would ever have a home like this, and Stan's family had reveled in that fact.

At the halfway point from the street to the house, Stan paused once more. As with the juncture of the driveway and the street, he sought out and found the Plexiglass cover that showed another section of PVC piping and a second green light.

Straightening up, he crossed the second line and moved toward the house. Every few steps, he saw the skeleton of a bird or a squirrel, sometimes that of a larger animal, either a fox or an opossum. Unfortunate creatures who had been chased into a place they normally would have avoided.

A place Stan did well to avoid.

Twenty or so feet from the wide front steps that led up to the broad porch, Stan came to a stop once more. When he moved again, it would be to retreat back toward the street and not further in.

He rested both hands on the stick's handle and waited.

She did not keep him waiting long.

From the right, a large rock hurtled towards him, narrowly missing his face as it passed in front of him.

Stan did not flinch. He had not done so since before he had left for the Army.

"Why are you here?" she demanded.

His great-aunt appeared and stepped out from his right, rage and hatred poisoning her once beautiful features.

"Philomena," Stan greeted, remembering his manners and bowing.

She hissed at him. "You foul this place with your presence, boy!"

"It is my responsibility as the last living member of this family to ensure the property's well-being," Stan reminded her.

"I take care of this house. Myself and no other," she snapped.

The dead woman drifted closer, her lower half hidden by the long bathrobe she wore.

Philomena had died in her sleep, suffocated with a pillow by her husband, who in turn suffered a fatal heart attack as he pressed down harder than he should have, just to be certain.

Stan's great-uncle had not stayed back, and for that, Stan offered up some small thanks to the universe. While the man was not nearly as bad as his wife, he was by no means a gentle soul.

Stan had hated them both.

"I see you have killed a few more animals," Stan observed, stepping off to the left. He followed a slim trail that was flanked on either side by

PVC piping filled with iron filings and rock salt.

"I wish they were you," Philomena replied. She grinned at him with a mouthful of cracked and crooked teeth. "I think of that as I squeeze the air from their little lungs."

"I am certain you do," Stan smiled. He moved at a slow pace, allowing himself the opportunity to look at each element of the house. His eyes sought out any siding that needed repair or windows that had broken. He missed nothing. The building was his home, regardless of whether he lived in it or in a room at Marilyn's.

The house was his. He had grown up in it, and he had suffered in it. More than a little of his blood had seeped into the wooden beams.

"Have you come here to kill yourself?" Philomena asked, keeping pace with him on the other side of the PVC pipe.

"Not yet," he answered.

"Will you ever?"

Stan considered the question, then replied, "If I do choose to end my life, yes, I will do so here. However, I will make certain you are not here at the time."

She stopped and glowered at him. "You cannot remove me from my home. It is me, and I am it. We are one and the same."

"Oh, I know," Stan nodded. "I will burn this place to the ground, and once it is gone, so too will you be. Then, in the ashes, I will stand and take my life."

"I won't let you," she snarled.

Stan frowned and looked at his great-aunt. The thin, almost gaunt woman who had tortured him for a decade was the incarnation of hatred. Stan never knew why she hated him, although he suspected it was because she had to take care of him after his parents' death. As a child and a young teen, he had feared her and his great-uncle. His body still bore the scars of their punishments.

But he knew she couldn't touch him, and he knew her strength was only enough to throw the occasional stone.

Stan walked between the PVC piping to give her a sense of control. To let her believe that she dominated this place still.

She knew nothing of the iron in his flesh, and he would keep that secret until the end.

"You may not want to let me," Stan told her. "But you will. You'll have no choice, and in the end, you'll suffer."

"I taught you about suffering," Philomena hissed. "But the lessons weren't done."

"Oh, they are. Now, if you don't mind, I would like to finish the inspection."

She called him several unpleasant names, but Stan ignored them. He walked the rest of the perimeter and was pleased to note that there was nothing out of the ordinary with the home at the time. He would check again in the following month if a bit of bad weather came down and treated the town roughly.

When Stan stood once more at the top of the driveway, Philomena came to a stop in front of him.

"One day," she told him, "these little lines of salt and iron will break, and I will come after you."

"That would be a pleasant visit," Stan replied smoothly. "However, I am not nearly close enough for you to do so."

A flicker of uncertainty passed across her face.

"Ghosts, for the most part, have a range limit," Stan explained. "If you travel more than a mile, you are usually dragged back to your item. One day, you might find out about the limit. I hope not, though. I would much rather see you trapped here until it's time for you to be truly and completely destroyed. Who knows, though, I might die before I ever decide to destroy this place. Wouldn't that be pleasant for you?"

"And what will happen to my house if you die, hmm?"

Stan bestowed upon her a cold, hard smile.

"One of my friends will come and burn it to the ground."

She sneered at him. "Watch yourself, boy. Just because you've imprisoned me here doesn't mean I don't know what's going on in town. People talk, and I listen. You're in a run for your money, although you don't know it. Not everyone here likes you. Certainly not the dead. What with your constant meddling. And for that, you're going to die sooner rather than later. My only regret is that I won't be able to watch it."

Stan shifted his attention from Philomena to the house.

"Wishing you were living there still?" she asked with a vicious grin.

"No," Stan confessed. "I am wondering how much kerosene it will take to burn it to the ground."

CHAPTER 10

SLOWING IT DOWN

"Now?" Omer asked.

"Now," Kenny confirmed.

Omer gave a short nod and walked away from Kenny's truck toward the factory. A few other workers left their vehicles, their attention on Omer, who waved at them all.

The others waved back. Every one of them.

They were all on board with the plan.

Or, at least, it seemed that way.

Kenny had his doubts about a couple of the guys on the permanent Saturday shift. Omer hadn't said anything about them, and Kenny knew it was because the man thought he could handle them.

In the old days, when you could take a subordinate out back and slap them around a little, Omer would have been right.

But these were different times. Different people. Some of the guys on second were college kids struggling to get a grip on reality after school. Others were people with habits to feed; gambling, alcohol, or any of a half dozen others they could find in Nashua.

Some would worry about their jobs, about getting fired, and not being able to collect unemployment benefits. Others would wonder if they could get a little extra cash out of it. Kenny knew that as soon as the slowdown was passed along the line, someone would come outside. A quick trip to their vehicle to make a private call to James.

Twenty-one minutes after the shift started, a middle-aged man came out the door. He was someone Kenny wasn't familiar with. A new hire for the Saturday and Sunday shifts.

Someone brought on by James.

Kenny shook his head. He hadn't thought James and Pettigrew might hire spies to work on the shifts. It would make sense, though, especially considering Pettigrew's business model. The man wouldn't be able to trust any of the old workforce, and he couldn't risk bribing any of them. A bribed man or woman might just turn around and go back to their coworkers with the proof.

No, your own inside man would be the way to go.

Kenny wondered how many other new hires were plants. It didn't matter, but he was curious.

Kenny watched the man walk to a battered, dull gray Honda Civic and then climb in, taking his cell phone out of his back pocket. As soon as the driver's side door closed, Kenny exited his truck.

He made a beeline for the Civic, doing his best to keep out of the line of sight offered by the vehicle's mirrors. When he neared the vehicle, he could see the man was focused on the factory as he held a cell phone to his ear. Kenny stepped up to the driver's side at an angle and heard the end of the conversation.

"Yes, sir, that's right," the occupant said. "There's a slowdown for each shift. They won't dip too far beneath normal production, but they are most definitely not going to meet Mr. Pettigrew's quota… No, that's all, sir. I have to go back in. Omer gave me permission to get my charger. He'll be suspicious if I take much longer… Yes, sir, I'll keep you informed."

For a moment, Kenny considered attempting to retreat but then decided against it. It didn't matter if the man saw him or not.

The door opened, its hinges complaining as the man stepped out, and then stopped, a look of shock and then feigned pleasantness as he saw Kenny.

"Hey, I didn't see you there," the man said, getting out of his car fully and closing the door. "Decided to work the Saturday shift after all?"

Kenny smiled. "No. I was just wondering how long it was going to take James to find out about our plan. A hell of a lot quicker than I thought, I'll give you guys that. Never even considered they'd bring in people to watch us."

The man smiled. "Got no idea about what you mean."

"I'm sure you don't," Kenny chuckled. He took his phone out and sent Omer a quick text.

Whoever came out to get their charging cable just ratted us out to James. Kenny hit send and then looked up to see the man still looking at him.

"You're going to want to be careful when you go in there," Kenny warned, putting his phone away.

"Why's that?"

"There are a few guys on the Saturday shift that enjoy their fights, and when Omer finishes telling them about you betraying everyone, well, they're going to line up to get their hands on you."

The man shook his head, a look of concern filling his face. "I don't know what you're talking about."

"I'm telling you right now," Kenny continued. "Some of those men are going to take you down to a storage room and beat you seven ways to Sunday. I don't know how much extra you're being paid to be a plant, but it's not going to be worth the abuse you'll take until this is over."

"Those hicks don't scare me," the man growled, his voice suddenly filled with venom.

"One or two of them shouldn't," Kenny agreed. "But when you get six or seven of those boys together, and they decide they're going to use you to sight their .22s with, you're going to be scared."

The man licked his lips and glanced at the factory.

"So, you've got two choices," Kenny told him. "You can go back into the factory and get a beating. I can guarantee you that. If you try to press charges, you'll go missing sometime in the next few weeks. And when I say missing, that's what I mean. There's a whole lot of forest around us, in case you haven't noticed, and these boys know where they could hide a body. Then, of course, there's choice number two. Get in your car and drive the hell away from here. I don't think you came to work here because you love Pettigrew or James. You came here for the money. Kind of tough to spend it if you're dead."

Without a word, the man climbed back into his car, closed the door and started the engine. Kenny watched the car pull out of the parking spot and speed out of the lot.

Shaking his head, Kenny walked toward the factory. He needed to tell Omer about the plant quitting so Omer could call and tell James.

✷ ✷ ✷

Ezra pinched the bridge of his nose.

It had already started, and the man Kenny had chased off was one of Ezra's resources.

Kenny would need to be taken care of. There was no other way around it. And it would have to be done sooner rather than later.

Ezra knew the steps he was taking were drastic, but there had never been as much money on the line as this. He had too much to lose, and he had no intention of losing it.

The waiter returned to his table and smiled. "Will you be having dessert, sir?"

"Please," Ezra nodded, returning the smile. "What do you have for cakes this evening?"

With a wide grin, the waiter cheerfully told him.

Death could wait.

Cake could not.

The room smelled of sweat, old beer, and hard work, and none of it was unfamiliar to Stan. He made his way through the packed dance floor, working his way to the edge until he spotted Adam sitting at a table close to the back corner.

Adam waved, and Stan returned the gesture. In a moment, he slid into the seat and saw that Adam had already ordered a pitcher of beer and a pair of mugs. With a grin, the younger man filled both.

"Here's to Mack and Marilyn," Adam toasted, and Stan joined him.

The beer had a strong taste, and Stan's reaction must have shown on his face.

Adam chuckled, raised his voice above the increasing din of the dance floor, and said, "Tyler's homebrew. Little hard."

"A little," Stan agreed and set his mug on the battered tabletop between them. "It is rather strange for me to be here."

"How so?" Adam asked, pouring a second glass for himself.

"Kenny informed me that it has been close to three years since I had any alcohol," Stan replied. "And the last drink was, in fact, here in Dow's."

Adam laughed and took a sip from his beer. "I guess it's appropriate that you're having a drink here, then."

Stan looked at the young man across from him and nodded. Adam was a much-changed man, and it had all started with a meal from Mack and a place to live from Marilyn.

"Mack and Marilyn have certainly done you well," Stan observed.

"So have you, Stan," Adam said. "You helped me, too."

Stan shook his head. "I appreciate you saying such a thing, Adam, but I do not believe it is true. Yes, you have helped me a bit around Marilyn's, but you have earned your place here in Mason."

"Stan," Adam began, leaning forward. "You helped me face the dead. And you're teaching me more about them every day. Yeah, Mack and Marilyn, they arranged the foundation for me, but you're building the house."

Stan nodded and let the subject fade away. For a short time, the two of them drank in silence, looking out over the dance floor and the people moving to some song Stan couldn't recognize. The temperature in the bar increased a few degrees, and Stan found it necessary to remove his suit coat. He took it off, folded it, and put it on the seat beside him. Stan removed his cufflinks, put them in his pocket, and then rolled his shirt cuffs up twice.

Adam, Stan noticed, was looking at the myriad of scars covering Stan's forearms.

"Did you have tattoos?" Adam asked, his tone one of surprise.

Stan looked at his forearms. He had, in all honesty, forgotten all about them.

"Yes," Stan answered. "I did."

"Do you mind if I ask what happened to them?"

Stan hesitated and then realized he had never talked to anyone other than Kenny about what had happened.

"I was in the Army," Stan explained. He looked down at his forearms.

"This one," he tapped his right arm. "I had the Army's emblem tattooed. And on my left, I had a radio in the center of a target with the letters RTO beneath it."

"Why a target?" Adam asked.

"I was a radio operator," Stan stated. "That meant in combat, I was a target. A bullet magnet. Kill the officer and the operator, and you effectively neutralize the team, if only for a short while."

"Did you have an accident?"

Flashes from the highway of death raced at him, and Stan stiffened unwillingly.

"Hey," someone said from the right, cutting off Stan's response. "How are you doing?"

Both he and Adam turned to see an attractive young woman dressed in a tight-fitting pair of jeans and a cropped flannel shirt staring at Adam. She was, without any doubt, well on her way to being drunk. Her black hair, highlighted with glimmering strands of metallic colors woven into it artfully, hung down about her shoulders.

"I'm doing okay," Adam smiled. "Better now, actually."

"That's what I like to hear," the girl grinned, and she sat down beside Adam, pressing herself against him. "So, what does a girl have to do to get a drink around here?"

Adam chuckled, topped off his glass and handed it to her.

"Thanks," she said with an exaggerated wink and took a sip. Her eyes widened, and she took a longer drink. "You bought the good stuff."

"I did," Adam nodded. "It's for my friend here."

The young woman glanced at Stan. "Hey, I think I know you."

"There is that chance," Stan admitted.

She squinted. "Yeah. I do, you came to my house, like, I don't know, ten years ago. Something bad was there."

Stan frowned, looked closer at the young woman and then nodded. "You are a Hemmings. I should have seen it in the line of your nose. You have your grandmother's features."

The young woman straightened up with pride.

"You must be Agatha," Stan continued. "Are you doing well?"

Agatha Hemmings glanced at Adam, let out a pleased laugh and nodded. "Damned right I am."

"Agatha!"

The anger in the voice kicked off every alarm in Stan, and he shifted his position in the bench seat, swinging his legs out so he sat facing the dance floor.

A trio of young men pushed their way through the crowd, and Stan tried to get a feel for them.

They were dressed comfortably in almost identical outfits. Like Agatha, they wore jeans and flannel shirts, albeit theirs were not cropped. On their feet, they wore working boots that had never seen a day of work and disturbingly stiff cowboy hats on their heads. Their belts were each emboldened with a large buckle; one man's bore a fish, the other a bear, and the last a stag.

Unlike Agatha, the men were not close to being drunk, nor did they look pleased to see Adam.

"Agatha, get away from him now," Fish snapped.

Agatha gave Fish a look that told Stan everything. He could see it as if playing on a projector before him. The young woman and Fish had broken up from a long and serious relationship. He was the one who had ended it, admitting to some act of infidelity he had been certain she would forgive.

Agatha had not forgiven, and she had called it off. Stan could imagine her emptying their shared apartment, her decision to go out and remind herself she was beautiful. She wanted to dance and have fun and to flirt with a man who was attractive. If the night led anywhere after that, she might be open to it, but she wasn't leading off with that intention.

Regardless of how things went with Adam, one fact was blatantly clear.

Agatha Hemmings wanted nothing to do with Fish, Bear, or Stag.

"Get over here now, Agatha," Fish snarled. "You're making a damned fool of yourself!"

"Leave me alone," she replied and picked up the glass of beer.

Fish stepped forward, and Stan stood up. Fish stopped and looked at him, bemusement on his face.

"What are you, his dad or something?" Fish asked the question, eliciting snickers from his compatriots.

Stan felt an old fire ignite in his belly, causing it to churn and twist. Shivers raced along his flesh, and he looked from man to man to man.

"The young woman wishes to remain at this table," Stan informed them. "Please leave her alone and allow her to enjoy the evening."

"Or what?" Stag asked.

Stan didn't respond.

For a moment, he stood in front of Fish, and then Fish tried to shove him aside.

It had been almost five years since Stan had fought someone, and that fight hadn't been pretty.

This one wasn't either.

Movements drilled into him a thousand times resurfaced, his mind making decisions quickly and at a subconscious level.

Stan brushed away Fish's attempt, caught the younger man's hand by the thumb and twisted it. A shriek of pain burst from Fish's mouth as Stan pushed the hand up the wrong way, driving the younger man to the floor. From his peripheral vision, Stan saw the other two men pause, then hurry toward him.

Without any hesitation, Stan brought his foot down on Fish's shoulder, dislocating it.

Stan let go of Fish's thumb and ducked below Bear's clumsy attempt at a haymaker. Two quick jabs to the kidney left Bear struggling for breath even as Stan stepped away from the man. As he did so, Stag tried to kick him, and Stan caught the younger man's foot. Stag's eyes widened, and then he howled with pain as Stan punched him in the side of the knee, dislocating it with the third punch.

Stan let go of Stag's leg and turned around to see Bear stumbling toward him. Stan opened his arms, caught the man in a bear hug, and then drove his knee into Bear's groin.

Gasping and retching, Bear fell away to the floor, and it was then that Stan realized Dow's was silent.

Looking around, he saw the crowd was looking at him. Some with looks of boredom, most with expressions of surprise. Stan realized the room was silent. Someone had turned off the radio.

"Stan."

He turned to face the bar and saw Tyler Dow standing behind the bar. "Sherrif will be here in a minute. You may want to get outside and wait for him."

"Of course, Tyler," Stan agreed, nodding. He returned to the booth, picked up his suit coat and offered up a soft "good evening" to Adam and Agatha before stepping over the moaning forms of the young men he had beaten.

The crowd parted to let him out, a few people complimenting him on his fighting. Stan accepted them with a polite smile, but he felt no joy over what he had done. He felt, instead, a sense of disappointment in himself. He could have defined the situation. That wouldn't have been any sort of an issue at all.

No, he had wanted to fight.

Stan left the bar and sat down on the curb. As he waited for the sheriff, he considered what he had done and what the trigger had been.

And then he realized it.

The scars. Talking about the scars had brought out the worst in him. He hated remembering how he had gotten the wounds, and despite the gifts the injuries had granted him, he still hated the memories of that day.

With a sigh, Stan rolled down his shirt sleeves, refitted the cufflinks, and then slid his suit coat on. He closed his eyes and listened to the night insects singing in the trees and wished he was home in bed.

CHAPTER 12

LOST AND FOUND

"Hello?"

Deputy Analise Pizarro looked up at the old woman standing in front of her. The stranger looked as though she had stepped out of a movie from the forties, and not a good one. Her face was haggard, her clothing ragged, and a strange sense of despair hung in the air around her.

"May I help you?" Analise asked.

"I found this," the woman replied, dropping a silver pin in the shape of the letter L on the counter. "I think it's important."

Analise picked it up and hissed, letting go of the painfully cold metal. She looked up at the woman and frowned.

The old woman was gone.

The phone rang, and Analise shook her head and answered the phone.

Sheriff Bowman stood in front of the cell door and looked in at Stan.

"You sure you're okay?" the sheriff asked.

Stan nodded as he sat down on the cot, setting the blanket and pillow down beside him. "I am quite sure, Sheriff."

"Want to tell me again what happened?"

Stan offered a slight smile. "I lost my temper. The young men looked to engage Adam in a fight. One of them was upset, and his friends were there to assist him with whatever rough justice they felt was necessary."

"That's what most of the people in the bar are saying, too," the sheriff said.

"How are the young men?" Stan asked, dreading the answer.

"Oh, they'll be here soon enough," Sheriff Bowman told him. "Two with braces to help with the dislocations, the third with a month's supply of icepacks."

Stan nodded.

"I'm putting the three of them in the larger cell across the way," the sheriff stated. "I don't want any grief between the four of you."

"I have no intention of causing any further disturbance," Stan remarked. "I regret what I have done."

"I know you do, Stan," Sheriff Bowman nodded. "I was surprised it had happened. It's been years since your last outburst, and this one wasn't as close to bad as the last one was. And I have to talk to those boys. They learned a hard lesson today, and I want to make sure they don't have to learn another later on."

"I will not go looking for them," Stan assured the man.

Sheriff Bowman chuckled. "Oh, I'm not afraid of that. I'm concerned they might try and fight you over tonight's scuffle. I don't want them seriously hurt."

The man was about to continue when the radio on his hip beeped. Sheriff Bowman unhooked it and said, "Go for the Sheriff."

Stan couldn't quite hear what the response was, but it didn't matter either way. He would sit in jail and wait until the sheriff told him what was happening.

"I'll be right up."

Sheriff Bowman stood up and nodded to Stan. "I'll be back down in a few minutes with company."

"I will be here," Stan replied, and the sheriff chuckled as he left.

Sheriff Paul Bowman had known Stan Owens for all of his life, and had thankfully only seen Stan lose his temper a handful of times. Considering the damage that had been done before, Paul wasn't sure he was ready to count the fight at Dow's bar as one of those times.

Paul walked out into the main area of the station and saw the three young men Stan had injured. They sat on a long, uncomfortable bench with secure ports for handcuffs, and each man was cuffed.

None of them looked happy. The worst of the three was the one who had suffered a terrible blow to the groin. That man's face was still pale, and with his free hand, he held a large ice pack against his injured body part.

Deputy Analise Pizarro handed Paul a clipboard and shook her head before walking away.

Paul scanned the comments from the ER doctor. They were succinct, sparse, and the last line said everything that needed to be said about Stan and his abilities.

Patients one and two sustained injuries that were close to permanently debilitating, while there was the very real possibility of the surgical removal of the testes to save patient three. They were lucky, Paul.

Paul knew it was more than luck.

It was Stan.

Stan had pulled back on every blow. If he hadn't, it would have been messy.

Paul drew a chair over to face the three men on the bench. He didn't know any of them personally. Their information showed they were seniors at Keene College, as was the woman they were trying to talk to.

Paul sighed and identified the men by their injuries.

"Kamden," Paul said, and the man with the damaged arm nodded.

"Caspian." The man with the injured leg grunted.

"And that leaves you, Jason," Paul finished.

Jason didn't respond at all, and Paul couldn't blame him.

Setting the clipboard down, Paul looked at each man in turn before stating, "You're all lucky."

The three men looked at him with disgruntled disbelief.

"It's true," Paul told them. "Even the ER doc said so. I know it, though, because I've seen Stan fight before, and it sure as heck wasn't pretty."

None of the men spoke.

"Now, I'm not interested in why you were trying to harass that woman," Paul informed them. "Couldn't care one bit, to be honest. I can tell you that it'll be a bad idea to try and speak with her again. And I can tell you, without any hesitation, that it would be in your best interest to avoid Stan Owens."

"Who's that?" Kamden asked.

"That is the man who beat you seven ways to Sunday," Paul answered.

Caspian muttered something and Paul glared at him until Caspian looked away.

"I know you think I'm just trying to keep you away from a townie," Paul said. "And in a way, you're right. I am trying to keep you away, but it's not for his safety. It's for yours."

Caspian snorted. "He's just an old man who'll get what's coming to him."

Paul shook his head. "He pulled his punches."

"What?" Jason whispered.

"He pulled them," Paul repeated. "If he'd put a little more oomph on the punch you got, it would have been bad."

"It was already bad!" Caspian snapped.

Paul picked up the clipboard and read aloud, "Patients one and two sustained injuries that were close to permanently debilitating, while there was the very real possibility of the surgical removal of the testes to save patient three."

Jason looked down at his feet, and Caspian's face paled.

Kamden licked his lips nervously. "He pulled his punches?"

"He did," Paul said and put the clipboard down again. "And I've seen when he doesn't. That's why I'm talking to you now. I don't want you looking for trouble because you will surely find it with Stan. Am I understood?"

The three men nodded, although Caspian was a little slower than his companions.

"Are we going to jail now?" Jason asked.

"For a bit," Paul answered. "Just to make sure you're all sobered up and calm before you leave."

Kamden cleared his throat and asked, "When do we talk to someone about bail?"

"You don't," Paul replied. "Stan's not pressing charges, and neither am I. But you are going to sit for a spell. Is that understood?"

The men nodded.

"Good," Paul sighed. "Let's get you in."

✳ ✳ ✳

Analise checked the footage again and still didn't see the woman who had come in and left the silver letter L on the counter.

There was nothing except static and a faint shadow on the tape, and for some reason, the sight of both left her feeling ill.

She picked up her radio and called for Paul.

"Go," he replied a moment later.

"You busy?" she asked.

"Bringing our three Road House specials to their cell," Paul answered. "Why?"

"Got something funny going on. I don't like it."

"Can't wait?"

"No," she answered.

"Copy."

Paul appeared a few minutes later, leading the trio of young men from the earlier fight into the room.

"What's going on?" he asked, stepping around the counter.

"Watch," she answered and played the tape for him.

Paul's brow furrowed, and he asked, "Can you play that back for me?" She nodded and did so.

"What is that?" Paul asked, pointing at the screen.

Analise looked and answered, "It's a pin. That one."

She nodded toward the pin. It lay on the lower portion of the counter, where she had dropped it only a few minutes earlier.

Paul reached out, touched it, and then snatched his hand away.

"That's not good," Paul muttered. "Listen, I'm going to get these three put away for the night, then I'll be back up. Don't touch that again, okay?"

"No problem," Analise told him. "It hurt the first time, I don't see a need to get hurt again."

Stan sat on his cot and listened as Sheriff Bowman brought the three younger men in and walked them to the larger cell across from his. He listened as the door opened and closed, the men silent as they settled in.

A moment later, the door to Stan's cell opened, and Sheriff Bowman motioned for Stan to exit.

Frowning, Stan did so. In a low voice, he asked, "Is there a problem, Sheriff?"

"Yes," Sheriff Bowman answered. "It's upstairs. Something's just not right, and it seems like it's up your alley. Follow me."

Stan did so, and in a minute, they stood at the front desk.

"Good evening, Deputy Pizarro," Stan greeted.

The younger woman smiled. "Good evening, Stan. You okay?"

"I am, thank you." He turned to face the sheriff. "What is it you wished me to look at?"

"That," Sheriff Bowman answered and pointed at a small silver L on the desk.

Stan picked it up, ignoring the bitter cold snapping at his fingers as he turned the silver over in his hands. "This is a haunted item."

"Can you read anything on it?" the sheriff asked.

Stan turned it over and read aloud, "There is the initial 'L' in script, followed by the name 'Westchester'."

Stan frowned and put the pin down, rubbing his hands against each other to chase away the cold. "Perhaps this belonged to Lotta Westchester. She is the only person I can think of."

"Someone left it here," the deputy stated, and both she and Sheriff Bowman looked at Stan.

"What was her appearance?" Stan asked.

Deputy Pizarro gave him a brief description.

"That is most assuredly Lotta Westchester," Stan remarked, and he rubbed his chin for a moment. "She was not overly fond of law enforcement."

"I'm the one who shot her son, Chad," Sheriff Bowman sighed. "Tried to run me down in that beat-up Ford he always drove."

"He wouldn't have really hurt you." Lotta Westchester stood by the exit, the fluorescent lights piercing her pale frame. As she grew more solid, the lights flickered. She took a step toward the sheriff, and Stan placed himself between the dead woman and her target.

"I do not believe that to be a true statement, Mrs. Westchester," Stan informed her.

"No?" she asked.

"No. I knew Chad well," Stan continued. "He most certainly would have killed Sheriff Bowman. And whoever was in the way. Chad was unreasonable when he was angry."

The dead woman snorted. "That's a lie."

"It is not," Stan replied. Then, he shrugged. "That is neither here nor there, though. Why are you here, Mrs. Westchester?"

The dead woman launched herself across the room toward Sheriff Bowman.

Stan threw his arm out, and Mrs. Westchester tried to race through him.

It didn't work.

Instead, she vanished.

Stan shifted and looked at Sheriff Bowman. "My coat, where did you put it?"

"My office," the sheriff replied, his face pale.

"Fetch it, if you would," Stan started, but before he could add why, Lotta Westchester reappeared, and she was not pleased.

"What in the hell did you do?" she snapped.

"I stopped you," Stan answered. "I thought that was obvious, Mrs. Westchester."

"Don't you go anywhere!" she yelled at Sheriff Bowman, but the man ignored her and hurried to his office. To Stan, she barked, "Don't interfere!"

Stan made no response, but when the dead woman tried to walk past him, he put out another hand. Once more, she vanished, but she was back a moment later.

With a furious scream, she took hold of a glass paperweight off the front desk and hurled it at Stan. He dodged to one side, but the paperweight clipped the side of his head, sending him to his knees and causing stars to explode across his vision.

The dead woman let out a howl of triumph, tore the keyboard off the desk, and stepped forward, smashing down onto Stan's back. He heard and felt the plastic crack and watched a pair of keys bounce along the tiled floor. She brought it back up again, and Stan lashed out with his hand. It passed through her leg, and the dead woman disappeared, the keyboard dropping onto his head.

"Stan!" Deputy Pizarro knelt beside him. "Are you okay?"

"I am," Stan lied. "She'll be back."

"She is," Mrs. Westchester hissed, and the telephone bounced off his back.

Deputy Pizarro pulled him back as the dead woman dragged the monitor up.

"You let me fix that Sheriff," Mrs. Westchester spat. "And you stay outta my way, Stanley Owens."

"Stan!" Sheriff Bowman called and tossed the suit coat toward him.

Deputy Pizarro caught it, handed it to Stan, and then managed to catch the monitor as Mrs. Westchester threw it.

With his head spinning, Stan dug his hand into the inner pocket and retrieved a small, lead-lined case. He struggled to his feet as the ghost backed away from him, rage and fear dancing across her aged features, and she bared her yellowed teeth at him.

"I'll kill you too, Stanley Owens," she snarled.

"Not today," Stan replied, keeping an eye on her as he staggered to the desk. He opened the case, then picked up the silver L. "But it is something we can discuss later."

He dropped the cold L into the case and then closed and locked it.

Mrs. Westchester vanished, and Stan collapsed.

CHAPTER 13
AN ACCORD

"You'll do it then?" Ezra asked.

Theo grunted, then nodded. "Aye. It'll be something new. Something different."

"I hope so," Ezra smiled. "I hope it is something you will enjoy."

"Me, too," Theo chuckled.

Ezra closed Theo's container, and the dead man vanished. Ezra made sure to secure the lock before sliding the container into his pocket, and then he left his suite of rooms. He went down to the nondescript Honda compact he had purchased and climbed in. The clothes he wore were uncomfortable, second-hand affairs that were ill-fitting and hid the true form of his body. Despite his discomfort, Ezra felt better knowing that all the little things he did, none of which he could have thought of on his own, would help shield him from any retribution.

As did the use of a ghost to do his work.

The last part brought a grin to his face as he started the engine. The car grumbled and complained, backfiring once before he shifted into gear and left the hotel parking lot by the service vehicle entrance. At a red light, he put an earbud into his ear and activated the map app on his burner phone. It registered his location and told him how to get to the neighborhood closest to Kenny's house. Ezra had gone so far as to pin a specific house, one that was for sale.

Ezra hummed to himself as he drove along, not minding the ride or the pleasant weather that came through the car's ventilation system. Soon enough, he turned onto the street where the property was and pulled the car to a stop in front of it. He glanced at it, confirmed he was where he needed to be, and then turned the engine off.

Leaving his phone in the car, Ezra got out and began to walk.

He had memorized the way to Kenny's, and it took him exactly four minutes to get to the woods behind the man's house.

He didn't try to push himself any further. He was as close as he needed to be.

Taking out Theo's container, he opened it and let the ghost out.

Theo glanced around at the woods and nodded with approval. "Been a long time since I really been out." The dead man shifted and looked at the house. "Is that where he lives?"

"Yes," Ezra confirmed.

"Do I do it tonight?"

Ezra shook his head. "Tonight is his AA meeting. He won't be home for some time. Just familiarize yourself of the house."

"Fair enough." Theo turned. "I'll let you know how it goes."

Ezra only had time to nod before the dead man faded away.

Humming once more, Ezra followed his trail back to his car.

Stan woke to the sound of buzzing in his ears and a throbbing in his head. He eased his eyes open and felt a sense of relief from the darkness around him.

He moved slightly on the bed, and the mattress creaked.

"You awake, Stan?" Sheriff Bowman asked.

"I am," Stan answered, and as he did so, a deep, uncomfortable pain sprang up in his back.

"Want some company?"

"Yes," Stan replied.

The cell door, which Stan realized was hung with a pair of thick blankets, opened just enough to allow Sheriff Bowman to slide into the room, pulling it closed quickly behind him.

"Darker than I thought in here," the sheriff remarked.

"And not dark enough right now," Stan muttered, rolling onto his back and staring into the darkness above him.

"How are you feeling?"

"Terrible."

"I can only imagine. I'd like to get you to the hospital sooner rather than later," Sheriff Bowman informed him.

Stan tried to frown, but a shot of pain through his brow stopped him. "We will see, Sheriff. Is everyone all right?"

"We are," Sheriff Bowman replied. "We still have Lotta in the box, too."

"I am more concerned with the amount of power she has," Stan said. "It is rare for a ghost to be so powerful as to manipulate their surroundings as if they were still alive."

"Yeah, well, it was pretty rotten watching you get beat like that," the sheriff admitted.

"It was," Stan smiled, "fairly rotten experiencing it."

Sheriff Bowman offered up a dry chuckle.

"Where is Deputy Pizarro?" Stan asked.

"Asleep in one of the interrogation rooms," the sheriff answered. "She didn't want to go home tonight."

"That is completely understandable," Stan remarked. "It is always difficult when dealing with the dead. Especially ones as violent as Mrs. Westchester."

"You know," Sheriff Bowman said after a brief pause, "I've seen you do a few things here and there, Stan. Watched you fight when you were younger. Seen how you can talk a dead man back into the netherworld. I never thought I'd see you fight a dead woman in the middle of the Sheriff's office."

"To be perfectly honest, Sheriff, I never had any plans to fight in a Sheriff's office."

"No," Sheriff Bowman chuckled. "I don't imagine you would."

"What was the damage?" Stan asked.

"Well, we'll need to get you x-rays before I can say anything," Sheriff Bowman began, and Stan chuckled. The sheriff frowned. "What? What is it?"

"I wasn't worried about myself," Stan admitted. "I am more concerned about the office and your staff. My body will heal, it always does. Computers, monitors, they do not."

"Well, let's leave it at this, Stan," the sheriff said. "Those are all covered. What isn't covered is you. I don't want to lose you, my friend. All right?"

"Yes," Stan sighed. "That sounds fine."

✳ ✳ ✳

Paul closed the door over and stood for a moment in the center of the room.

"Um, Sheriff?"

Paul looked over and saw Kamden standing in their cell. The man's two companions were asleep.

"What can I do for you, Kamden?" Paul asked.

"Can I ask what happened?" The young man cleared his throat. "I heard some stuff. I mean, we all did, but they went to sleep. They weren't too worried about it."

"They didn't have to worry about it," Paul told him. "But I doubt they weren't worried because they were confident in my abilities as a sheriff."

Kamden shook his head.

"It's fine," Paul said. "Now, do you really want to know what happened, or are you content with just making up stories about what it could have been?"

"They are," Kamden answered, nodding towards his sleeping friends. "I want to know. I, I need to know."

Paul nodded, grabbed a chair from an empty office, and brought it over to the cell Kamden shared with his friends. Sitting down, Paul looked at the younger man.

"Do you believe in ghosts?"

"Kind of," Kamden answered. "I mean, I know there are ghosts. It's just I've never actually seen one. At least, I don't think I have."

"You're not missing anything," Paul told him. "Well, some ghosts are violent, and others aren't. Some can touch you, but most can't. Not in the way you might think. I only say this because of all the years I've seen Stan work. What you heard tonight was Stan fighting a ghost."

Kamden's eyes widened, and Paul nodded.

"Yes," Paul continued. "It was a little shocking. If I hadn't seen it, I don't think I would have believed it."

Kamden looked to the blanket-covered door of Stan's cell. "Is he okay?"

"As well as can be expected. The biggest challenge now will be getting him to see a doctor. Think you can try and sleep?" Paul asked.

"Is it safe?"

Paul nodded. "Probably the safest it can be. Stan took care of the ghost, and now he's resting. I don't think anything will happen."

"Are you sure?" Kamden asked, and Paul could see the fear creeping into the young man's eyes.

"That we're safe here with Stan?"

Kamden gave a short nod.

"Without a doubt," Paul assured him. Standing up, he moved the chair back to the office. "I'm staying here the rest of the night, and so is the deputy. I'll be down periodically to check on Stan, but if you get worried, just give me a holler. I'll hear you. The station isn't that big."

Paul waited until Kamden sat back down on a bunk before he went upstairs. He walked around the station and took stock of the damage once more. It would cost a bit to pay for the broken items, and to bring in a repair team to make sure all the electricals and such were fine. Paul didn't mind, though.

It had to be done, and there was no other way of looking at it.

He walked over to check on Analise and found her asleep on a folding cot, covered in a blanket. A sudden weariness slipped over him, and Paul fought it off. He didn't want to sleep, not yet. There was too much to do.

He walked to the evidence room, keyed himself in, and then went to the safe. He opened it and saw the small box Stan had put Lotta in. Paul looked at it for almost a minute before he secured the safe once more.

He exited the evidence room, made certain the front desk area was cleaned up, and hoped nothing happened between now and the start of the midnight shift.

Adam sat with Agatha Hemmings, who was asleep, leaning against him. A small line of drool spilled out of the side of her mouth and darkened his sleeve. Adam found he didn't mind. Not at all.

The waitress came over and looked at the two of them. "You two okay?"

Adam nodded. "She's a little worse for wear right now."

"No more drinks?"

Adam chuckled and shook his head. "No. But if we could get a plate of fries and a couple of Cokes, that would be great. I'm going to try to wake her up in a minute. See if eating something will help."

The waitress smiled at him. "That's doable. Let me know if you need me to call her sister for her."

"I will," Adam said.

When the waitress walked away, Adam glanced at his phone. There was no call from the sheriff and no call from Kenny. He looked out to the dance floor, and the memory of the fight flashed before him.

He had seen fights before, but nothing like that. Stan, who didn't look like he could hurt a fly, had been the epitome of controlled violence. Every strike had been delivered with precision. Adam had watched enough action movies and reality military shows to know how skilled someone had to be to do the damage Stan had without killing someone.

The phone buzzed, and Adam picked it up.

Nothing. Just an advertisement.

He sighed and put the phone down just as Agatha snorted and sat up. She looked around, a bemused expression on her face. She looked at him, squinted, then smiled. The smile faded as she realized she had been asleep.

"Oh, man," she moaned. "How much did I drink?"

"I don't know," Adam answered. "But there're fries and a couple of Cokes coming our way."

"Rum and Cokes?" she asked with a sour frown.

Adam laughed and shook his head. "No. Not at all. Just regular Cokes. Thought that would be a good way to get sobered up."

Agatha looked around and asked, "Where's Stan?"

"That is an interesting story," Adam replied.

The waitress arrived with a plate of fries and the two Cokes.

"Hey, MJ," Agatha greeted.

"Hey, yourself," MJ answered. "You feeling better?"

"Yeah."

The waitress looked at Adam and said, "You were lucky Stan was here. That could have gone sour for you. Let me know if you need anything."

Adam nodded and watched the waitress leave.

"Any news from Stan?" Agatha asked.

"Nope," Adam answered. "But knowing Stan, I'm sure he's fine."

Chapter 14
The Workshop

"How are you feeling?" Marilyn asked, closing the door behind her.

"Exhausted," Stan informed her. "And I am extremely sore."

"You look it," Marilyn nodded, taking his coat from him and hanging it in the hall closet. "Step into the kitchen, Stan. I've prepared a bit of tea for you."

Stan smiled his thanks and followed her into the kitchen.

The room, like the rest of the house, gleamed with cleanliness. A small table, crafted from chrome and red vinyl and flanked by two chairs of matching heritage, stood off to the right. A cup of tea awaited at one seat, steam rising from it. Marilyn motioned for him to sit, and he did so. A tremble rippled through him, and he tried to hide it.

"Was that from being tired or from the beating you took?" she asked.

"I do not know," Stan admitted. "I suspect it is a fine mixture of the two."

Marilyn took the seat across from his. "Sheriff Bowman told me this was the worst thing he had ever seen."

"It was a terrible experience," Stan nodded. "I confess, I would like to avoid any more such as that one."

"Here's hoping you do," she replied and lifted a glass of water.

Stan murmured his agreement, lifted the teacup, and sipped at the perfectly brewed drink.

They were silent for a moment together.

"Adam was not involved," Marilyn stated.

"You are correct."

Another pause hung between them.

"Adam informed me that the men you fought with were interested in him," she said.

"They were," Stan agreed. "It was more because Agatha Hemmings was interested in Adam."

"Ah," Marilyn nodded. "That would make more sense. And it would explain why there was a hint of perfume about him."

"Is he still sleeping?" Stan asked.

"He only just went to bed," Marilyn informed him. "He was pacing about the kitchen, anxious to see you. It took some convincing to finally make him get some rest."

"I am glad you did," Stan told her. "I appreciate his concern, but he needs to sleep. He works hard."

Marilyn raised an eyebrow. "Stan Owens, you work hard as well, and, what's more, we all know it."

Stan murmured his thanks and finished his tea.

"What business are you about today?" she asked, standing up and removing the cup and saucer from the table.

"I will go into the barn," Stan answered. "I am short on boxes for items. It would be unfortunate to run out of them. I have had to make do with rock salt before, and it is always a harrowing business."

Marilyn nodded, placed the dishes in the sink and turned to face him. Worry was etched around her eyes, and the furrows of her brow had deepened.

"You will be careful, won't you?" she asked.

"I am always careful, Marilyn," Stan said. "There is too much to do for me to be foolish."

"You are too loved to be careless," Marilyn informed him. "This town needs you. I will fetch you at noon for lunch."

Marilyn left the dishes in the sink, an abnormal act on her part, and exited the kitchen. Stan remained for a few minutes longer, trying to understand how the town needed him and how he was too loved.

He couldn't make sense of either. How could one be too loved, and how could a town need one person?

Stan shook his head, confused, and stood up. He exited the kitchen, still pondering the questions, and went to the back hall. He left the house, took the old granite steps down to the back path, and followed it to the large red barn that had, decades earlier, housed horses and wagons. Before the wooden floor had gone soft with age, members of Marilyn's family had parked their cars in the barn.

But then the earth and the elements had assailed the structure, and they had made the floor unsafe for any sort of vehicle.

When Stan reached the barn, he went around to the side, where a small door led the way into what had once been the harness and tack room. Now, it contained woodworking tools, sheets of lead, and a good supply of strong wood. It was here, removed from everyone else, that Stan crafted the small boxes he used to store the haunted items of the dead.

Over the years, he had learned that most items, not all but most, were small and could fit in boxes ranging in size from a jeweler's box for a ring to an old-fashioned pencil box for school.

He had discovered that not only were the boxes necessary for the successful storing of an item, but the crafting of the boxes was soothing. When he built them, he did not think of the highway.

When he built them, he could not smell the corpses.

Stan turned on the lights in the room, flicked the heat switch into the upright position, and took his leather apron off its hook. As he slipped it over his head and then tied it around his waist, he pushed open an inner door and walked into a narrow hallway. His shoulders brushed the walls as he moved along the dim length, his shoes whispering across the aged floor. At the far end, he came to another door. Unlike the rest of the structure, this was new, a thick, steel door lined with lead and iron filaments. An electronic keypad was the only way to unlock it, and if power was cut, deadbolts clicked into place on all four sides. When power was restored, it took a full twenty-four hours for access to be granted.

Stan had designed the parameters of the system himself, and certain members of Mason had helped fund it.

They knew what was beyond the door.

They knew what was locked away and, more importantly, they knew why.

Stan typed in the passcode, the latch released, and the door opened.

He entered the room, and soft motion sensor lights sprang to life as he came to a stop just inside the doorway. He looked about the room at the narrow shelves that lined the walls. Hundreds of boxes, all of them crafted by his hands, stood on the shelves. Each box was numbered, and each number corresponded to an entry in a handwritten catalog he kept in the room on top of an old combination school desk and chair. The entries were as complete as he could make them, with the names, dates, and all information possible entered on each page.

Stan removed the small box containing Lotta's silver L and brought it to the desk. He sat down, opened the notebook, and wrote quickly in short block letters. When he finished, he wrote the number for the entry onto the box and then carried it to the shelves. He placed it to the right of the previous number and then stepped back, suppressing the urge to double-check that the box was secure. He knew it was. She would have made every effort to stop him.

Stan turned around and left the room, closing it and listening as it automatically secured itself.

A strange itch settled in at the base of his skull, and he considered the curious fact that Philomena had known about Lotta. Either knew about her or knew something was up.

He would need to speak with her again, but he was tired, and it would be unwise to approach Philomena if he were not at the top of his game.

CHAPTER 15
REMINISCING

"You were fighting again."

Stan glanced over at Kenny, nodded, then turned his attention back to the sunset.

The two men sat in chairs against the back of the barn.

"I talked to Paul about it," Kenny continued. "He says you went easy on the boys."

"Yes."

"He also said that he told them," Kenny added.

Stan looked at him. "I did not know that."

Kenny nodded. "Yup. He wanted to make sure they didn't try and do something foolish, like go after you."

Stan closed his eyes for a moment. "No, that would have been a poor decision on their part."

Kenny snorted.

"What?" Stan asked.

"That's quite the understatement," Kenny observed, and Stan shrugged.

They were silent for a moment, and then Kenny asked, "This is an impolite question, Stan, but I'm curious, do you ever feel bad about what you did?"

"When I was younger?"

"Yes."

"Occasionally, I do," Stan stated. "But it is generally only regarding one or two instances, and certainly not all of them."

"I'm curious," Kenny said. "Which one bothers you the most?"

Stan forced himself to remember. "Jordan. Jordan Haynes."

Kenny nodded. "Tell me about it."

Stan shifted his position in his chair and looked at Kenny. "All of it?"

"All of it."

Stan cleared his throat. "What purpose does this serve?"

"Just trust me, Stan."

"Fine." He took a deep breath and focused on the memory.

"It was after I got home from Walter Reed Hospital," Stan began. "I was not in the best of shape, mentally. Physically, I was better than I had been despite the amount of shrapnel still in me. But I was drinking. Heavily. Whenever I could. I was still coming to grips with the fact that I could see the dead. That I could speak with them."

Stan paused.

"Did you ever see the dead down at Walter Reed?" Kenny asked, his question gentle.

"It was the first place I saw them," Stan answered. "Perhaps the best place for me to do so. There were several members of the staff who were, well, for lack of a better word, sensitive to the presence of the dead. None of them, however, could see the dead as I could."

"And you still weren't dealing with it well," Kenny finished.

"No, I certainly was not." Stan looked at the scars on the back of his hands and then back to the horizon. "I did not want to see the dead. Not here. Not at home. And yet, there they were. They did not stop hounding me. I did not know what to do about them. I could not think clearly, and so I made it even more difficult to think. I went to Dow's and drank. Day in and day out. Then, one day, Jordan Haynes decided to make a comment about me. More about the fact that I was still healing from my scars. He suggested that rather than triggering a boobytrap, I managed to somehow injure myself through stupidity. I was not in the mood that day. Well, less than usual, I should say."

"Was he a threat to you?"

The question caught Stan off guard.

"No," he answered. "Not in the slightest. Jordan was a large man, yes, but he mistook his size for an ability to fight. Which was not the case."

"And can you fight, Stan?" Kenny's voice was low, hard.

"I can fight," Stan replied without hesitation. "I can fight without mercy."

"And did he receive any mercy the day you fought him?"

The question brought Stan back to the memory of that day. He could smell the night air and the heavy exhaust on the cool breeze. He heard the rumble of engines and saw the lights of the cars and the pickups parked in Dow's lot.

And he saw Jordan Haynes lying on the cracked asphalt in front of him. The man's eyes were already swelling, his mouth bleeding. The damage, Stan would later learn, was far more extensive. He had, in fact, broken several of his own fingers punching Jordan in the head.

"No," Stan answered. "I did not show him any mercy, and I should have."

"Easy to say with the fight in the past," Kenny stated. "Harder in the moment. I want you to understand that, Stan. I want you to be able to see how you've grown. If this were twenty years ago, all three of those young men would be in the hospital for a long time. You've grown. Matured, really. I don't want you to come down hard on yourself for the fight, okay?"

Stan nodded.

"So, other than the fight and Lotta making an appearance, what else have you heard?"

"Adam spoke to me of a dead boy he saw," Stan replied.

"Ghost or a real body?" Kenny asked.

"A ghost," Stan stated and repeated to Kenny what Adam had told him about the farm and the orchard.

Kenny frowned. "Shouldn't be any ghosts there. Not unless someone died a hell of a long time before my mother was born. I swear there wasn't a bit of gossip she didn't know or a skeleton in someone's closet she wasn't intimately familiar with. That woman could ferret out a piece of information like no one else."

"There was something else, too," Stan added.

"What's that?"

"Philomena."

Kenny looked surprised. "What were you doing talking to her?"

"She made an appearance as I was checking on the house."

"I told you not to do that without me," Kenny chided. "Or at least with Adam now. She was a nightmare when she was alive, Stan. She's hell on wheels now that she's dead."

"I keep her contained as much as possible," Stan reminded his friend.

"That doesn't mean she doesn't get the news, you know that." Kenny shook his head. "Let's hope she doesn't take an interest in Adam or anything else going on in town right now. It won't work out for you, and I doubt the town will see any benefit from it."

"No, it would not."

Kenny sighed. "What are your plans tonight? More fights at Dow's?"

Stan smiled and shook his head. "I will go to bed soon. I have a terrible feeling there is a great deal of trouble heading our way, and I would like to be well-rested for it. What about you, my friend?"

"I'm finishing up a new series about the Old West," Kenny answered. "Pretty good. Next part is on Clint Eastwood and the Man with No Name movies. I'm looking forward to it."

Stan, who no longer had any sort of patience for movies, could only nod.

As Kenny got to his feet, Stan did the same.

"Get some rest," Kenny said. "If you're right about there being trouble on the way, give me a holler. You know I'll come running."

"I will, Kenny," Stan assured his friend. "Enjoy your show."

Kenny chuckled, stretched and added, "I love Westerns, you know."

"Why is that?"

"Because the good guy always wins. What could be better than that?"

Stan shook his head. "I do not know."

Kenny laughed and waved. "Okay. I'll stop by soon."

Stan returned the wave and then brought the chairs back into the barn. There was a chance of rain overnight, and he disliked having to dry the chairs off.

CHAPTER 16
UNWANTED GIFT

Ezra squatted down, opened the container and released Theo.

The dead sailor appeared a moment later, balanced curiously, as always, on his one good leg. Ezra wondered, for a moment, if the ghost still felt the pain of his fatal injury.

It was a question that deserved to be asked and answered.

But not tonight.

Kenny at the factory had proven to be too difficult. Far more difficult than anyone else at any of the other establishments Ezra had taken over.

Ezra had been warned by other businessmen who had investments and interests in New England.

The men and women in his small sphere of influence had stated that the workers of New England were a challenge, and they hadn't been wrong. They had also informed him that his normal techniques, strong-arming and blackmailing, wouldn't work with the sturdy folk of New England. The workers were obstinate, well-informed of each other's secrets, and more than willing to butt heads together.

Ezra didn't inform his colleagues that he was going to be working out new techniques to encourage good behavior. Most wouldn't have believed him, and those who did would want to know too much.

Ezra disliked sharing information.

"Is it for real tonight?" Theo asked. "Or is it another dry run?"

"Tonight is the real deal," Ezra answered. "Remember, it needs to look like a suicide."

"I can do that," Theo smiled. "I've been practicing."

"I know," Ezra nodded. "I saw the nooses you made. Well done, by the way."

The dead man grinned with pride.

"Have you found anything you could use in the house?" Ezra asked.

"Yes," Theo confirmed. "There are a few ties in his closet."

"Good."

Ezra looked at Kenny's house, where the lights remained off. Soon, the sun would finish its descent, and the night would settle firmly upon Mason.

"When should I do it?" Theo asked, interrupting Ezra's thoughts.

"I would think as soon as possible," Ezra replied. "We can't have him in his undergarments looking as though he'd been dragged from bed."

Theo grumbled in agreement.

"The suicide theory will be more palatable if he looks as though he was making a conscious decision," Ezra stated dryly.

"I know," Theo muttered. "I'll do it as soon as I can then."

"Good." Ezra glanced at the fading light. "I need to make it back to my auto. I'll return in the morning."

"Don't worry," Theo grinned. "The job'll be done right."

"I'm sure it will," Ezra nodded.

The ghost faded from view, and Ezra left. He picked his way along the path. The trail, which cut through the woods, was well-traveled where he was, and he hoped that the police would have no need to search for any outside evidence.

If everything went as planned, then Theo would succeed in making Kenny's death appear to be a suicide by hanging.

Should the dead man fail, however, then the police might take it into their minds to look for someone who had a hand in Kenny's death. It might lead them to the supposition that someone assisted with the suicide, but it shouldn't lead to Ezra.

If need be, he would buy the evidence away from the police and destroy it. But that was an emergency plan, one he hoped never to put into play.

Humming to himself, Ezra moved away from Kenny's at a steady pace. He wanted to be as far from the scene of action as possible. Preferably in the comfort of his suite at the hotel. Perhaps even with a masseuse to work out some of the knots in his shoulders.

As Ezra walked, he wondered if the hotel had a masseuse on staff and, if not, where he might find one with a decent reputation.

CHAPTER 17
INVOLUNTARY ACTS

Kenny wanted a drink.

The simple fact of the matter was, like many alcoholics, he always wanted a drink. Some days were worse than others, and some were better.

This evening was not a better one.

Despite his confidence regarding the slowdown at the factory, Kenny had a nagging worry that some sort of violence would take place. He didn't mind if it was focused on him, and he knew it would be, but a worrisome fear plagued him that someone blameless would receive his punishment.

Kenny shook free his house key, climbed the steps to the porch and unlocked the side door, stepping into the darkness of his kitchen. His free hand found the light switch, and he flipped it up with an easy motion. He had lived in the house for forty-one years. He knew every creak and groan, and he knew exactly where to find each room's switches.

He closed and locked the door behind him, went to the sink and drew a glass of water from the tap. Without thinking, he drank the contents with one gulp and then returned the glass to its place. He made himself a peanut butter and banana sandwich on toast and carried it along with a fresh glass of water into his den. Once he was settled into his recliner, he balanced the plate on his knees and turned on the television.

The seven o'clock news came on, and he let the remote drop into the outer pocket of his recliner. He took his first bite of the sandwich, settled in, and listened as the news anchor droned on about stories out of Boston and Concord.

Kenny was halfway through the sandwich when the lights flickered several times and went out, along with the television.

Kenny muttered under his breath, set the plate aside and got to his feet. Before bothering with the circuit breaker, he went to the front window and peered out to see if the rest of the neighborhood was out of power.

It was not.

Kenny turned away from the window and caught a glimpse of movement by the stairs.

He froze, listened, and waited. In the stillness, he heard the rattle of a lamp on the second floor.

The rattle of one particular lamp.

Someone was in his room, and they had bumped into the bed table, disturbing the delicate balance of the antique light stationed there.

Anger surged within him, and Kenny made his way to the stairs, instinctively avoiding the loose boards that would alert the intruder to his arrival. He knew the stranger was there for him, not to rob but to intimidate. And the notion that Pettigrew thought he could do such a thing enraged Kenny.

Reaching the second floor, he kept to the left side of the hall, approaching his bedroom. When he came abreast of his open doorway, he paused, let his eyes adjust to the dim light slipping in through the window shades, and sought the intruder.

Nothing. Nothing except the lamp on his bed table, which stood in the wrong position.

Someone was in the room.

Kenny shifted his attention to the closet, the door open as always. There was nowhere to hide in it, the closet too small for anyone to stand and not be seen.

That meant alongside the bed, where there were too many boxes tucked beneath it.

Kenny slipped off his belt, wrapped a bit of it around his fist and let the heavy buckle, shaped like an American eagle, swing freely.

Whoever the intruder was, he was going to suffer for his trespassing, and he'd carry a message back to Pettigrew.

Kenny stepped into the doorway.

"I know you're in here," he stated, pitching his voice low. "You'll save yourself a world of hurt if you stand up and come out where I can see you."

Not a sound came from the room. Neither recognition of him having spoken nor the noise of someone getting to their feet.

Kenny stepped further into his bedroom, his grip tightening on the leather belt.

"Okay," Kenny shrugged. "Have it your way."

He walked around the foot of the bed and came to a stop.

No one was there.

A heartbeat later, he felt cloth snap around his neck.

He thrust his free hand up, trying to catch the noose before it tightened, but only his index and middle fingers managed to get in. Kenny swung the belt backward and did nothing more than overextend his arm and strike himself with the buckle against his back.

The unseen assailant pulled on the noose tighter, and Kenny dropped the belt. He tried to twist around, but he found himself jerked to the floor, his back thudding on the hardwood and causing him to lose his grip. Clawing at the noose, Kenny found no purchase.

The noose was yanked up, and something cracked in Kenny's neck. He lost all feeling in his extremities, and the world faded around him.

CHAPTER 18
AN UNWANTED INTERRUPTION

Stan sat in his room, on his bed, and tried to concentrate. His sleep had been populated solely with nightmares, and while he couldn't remember them, he hadn't slept well. He felt uneasy, as though something unpleasant was waiting for him downstairs.

A knock on his door interrupted his thoughts, and Stan said, "Come in."

When the door opened, Marilyn stood in the hall, a sad look on her face.

Frowning, Stan got to his feet. "What is it?"

"Sheriff Bowman is here," she explained. "He would like to speak with you."

Stan nodded and hurried out of the room, Marilyn following behind him. He found Sheriff Bowman in the kitchen, his hat in his hand. The sheriff looked at him with concern and asked, "Stan, did you hear from Kenny yesterday?"

"He came to visit me. That was around sundown. I have not heard from him since."

Sheriff Bowman sighed. "Sounds about right."

"What is going on with Kenny?" Stan asked.

"Looks like he tried to kill himself last night," the sheriff explained. "Didn't quite work. Well, not in the way he wanted. The doctors say he won't survive. They have him on life support right now until they can find a next of kin."

"Why would he kill himself?" Stan asked, stiffening. His hands trembled slightly. "That does not make any sense."

"Most of the time, suicides don't make sense," Sheriff Bowman stated, his voice gentle. "The people that commit suicide, or who make a genuine effort, well, they mask their emotions. We don't see how bad they're hurting inside."

Stan didn't argue. He knew he would gain no ground doing so. "Tell me, please. Where did this occur?"

"At his home."

"How did you find out?" Stan asked.

"One of the shift leaders at his job was supposed to have coffee with Kenny today," Sheriff Bowman explained. "When he knocked on the door, and Kenny didn't answer, he got worried. Kenny's no spring chicken. We got the call for a health and welfare check, and I was the one who went in. Glad I was, too."

"How did he try?" Stan asked. "Did he use his Colt?"

Sheriff Bowman shook his head. "No. He used a tie."

Stan frowned. "A tie?"

"A necktie," the sheriff nodded. "Made a noose, looped one end around his neck, the other around the overhead light in his bedroom. The light's little chandelier was secured to a crossbeam, but not that secure. It came right out of the ceiling, but not before he fractured a couple of vertebrae in his C-spine."

Stan took a deep breath. "Thank you for informing me, Sheriff Bowman."

"Are you going to be alright, Stan?" the sheriff asked.

"Yes," Stan replied. "Although I am deeply saddened. If you do not find any next of kin, please tell me."

"Sure thing," the sheriff nodded. "Marilyn, thank you."

"Of course," Marilyn replied.

Stan watched as she walked Sheriff Bowman to the backdoor, and when she returned, Marilyn asked, "Would you like some tea, Stan?"

He hesitated, then nodded.

* * *

By the time he finished his tea, Stan had formulated a plan.

He knew something was wrong with Kenny's situation. Regardless of what the sheriff said, Kenny would not have killed himself. The man had fought too long and too hard to remain sober. If anything had gone wrong, he would have plunged back into alcohol before killing himself.

After informing Marilyn that he was going for a walk, Stan left the house with a quick step. He wanted to get to Kenny's home as soon as possible, and he did not want to have to ask anyone for a ride. The fewer people who knew he was going, the better. Despite his friendship with Kenny, people would think it odd if Stan was suddenly in the man's home.

And he needed to be there. He needed to see what had happened.

He did not know Kenny's house well, but he knew Kenny.

First, Kenny would not have hung himself. The man had nearly been choked to death as a boy, and the memory of it haunted him. Second, Kenny, if it came down to it, would have started drinking. And, third, if the drinking would not have been the answer, he would have used the Colt .45 he kept in a box beneath his bed.

If it had come to the third option, Kenny would have killed himself in the bathroom. Specifically in the tub so as not to make a mess for anyone who found him. It was a subject of conversation that had come up once or twice before as he and Kenny had pondered life.

It took Stan thirty-seven minutes and twenty-nine seconds to reach Kenny's home.

There was no police presence. There was no crime scene tape.

Nor were there any curious neighbors. Kenny's street was sparsely populated, and the folks who lived on it had a tendency of minding their own business. Only towards the center of town did Mason residents begin to really dig into one another's lives.

Stan walked past Kenny's home, turned left a short distance after, and then followed a rough path to the back of the house. He crossed the yard, the grass still damp with the morning dew, and found the backdoor locked. He pulled out the spare key from its hiding place behind a loose board and let himself in.

He passed through a coat room, opened a door, stepped into the kitchen, and came to a stop.

A dead man stood in the doorway, his back to Stan.

The ghost was not Kenny's since Kenny was, as far as Stan knew, still alive. The dead man turned and saw Stan, but he made no gesture, did not speak.

Stan frowned.

"What are you doing in my friend's home?" he demanded.

The ghost didn't respond, although a look of incredulity spread across his face.

"I am speaking to you," Stan explained. "I can see you there, in your peacoat with your burns. Tell me why you are in my friend's house."

At this, the dead man's eyes widened. He paused, then began to move away.

"Where are you going?" Stan snapped, following the ghost. "Where do you think you can go? Are you the one who has tried to murder my friend? Speak to me!"

The ghost turned and bolted. It rushed up the stairs, and Stan followed. A second later, he watched as it raced out a second-floor window to the grass below. The dead man hurried into the woods, and Stan lost sight of him.

Stan retreated to Kenny's bedroom and saw the disarray and debris of the hanging light.

Kenny would have known the light wouldn't have held his weight.

Kenny didn't try to kill himself.

The ghost had tried to kill him and failed.

Stan left the bedroom and returned to the room where the ghost had escaped. Somewhere in the woods beyond, the dead man waited. Whatever object he was attached to was there, and Stan would need to find it.

But he would need supplies first.

Supplies and Adam.

CHAPTER 19
A GOOD WORKER

"Is he dead?" Ezra asked, standing in front of Theo in the woods.

"Not quite," Theo admitted. "He isn't going to get better, though. I heard some of the people talking when they came and took him away. Something broke in his neck, and I heard it when we were fighting, too."

"Does it at least look like he tried to kill himself?" Ezra kept his anger in check, waiting for the answer.

The dead man chuckled and nodded. "Looks like he made a bad job of it. I used a tie, then managed to get it tied off to the overhead light. When I let go, it pulled the whole thing down on top of him."

The anger eased out of Ezra, and a broad smile filled his face.

"That, Theo, is wonderful news. And you said he's fatally injured."

"Yup," Theo stated. "They don't think he'll last long."

"Good. Very good. No other trouble?"

"There was," Theo said, and Ezra frowned.

"How so?"

"Someone came into the house after everyone was gone. I was in there, minding my own business, and this stranger comes into the kitchen. I didn't think he could see me or anything, so I stayed still," Theo explained.

"He could see you?" Ezra asked.

Theo nodded. "And I was trying not to be seen. He called me out, though. Demanded to know if I had something to do with his friend. I took off running, and he chased me. I jumped out of the house and came back here. He finally left, but I think he'll probably be coming back.

Doesn't strike me as the type of guy who gives up."

Ezra's frown deepened. "That's an unpleasant complication. I hope this is the last we hear of him, but I will have to make preparations. Just in case."

Theo nodded. "Well, what's next, boss?"

"I have another worker who is angry. Evidently, he's the man who found Kenny. I'd like to take care of this fellow as well if you're feeling up to it."

"I am," Theo grinned.

"Good."

Ezra bent down, picked up the button, and put it away.

Omer poured himself another shot of rum, added some Coke to it, and knocked it back. His hands trembled. He'd seen a few things in his time, but for some reason, the sight of Kenny being rolled away on a stretcher was a little too much.

Sure, Kenny had been old and should have retired, but the man had always given off the air of being Superman, like there was nothing in the world that could hurt him.

Why would he have tried to kill himself? It didn't make any sense, and it made Omer nervous as hell.

It made him think someone was trying to send a message to the workers.

Omer reached for the rum, hesitated, and then lowered his hand. He thought hard about who might be behind the attack if it was, actually, an attack. It couldn't be James. The man had the spine of a worm. It might be Pettigrew, the new owner, but Omer had never met a member of upper management, let alone an owner, who was willing to get their hands dirty.

If it was someone sent to put some fear into the employees, it was a hired gun.

The idea of a mercenary helped Omer relax. A hired gun meant the man or woman would have no loyalty to anything other than money, and Omer had a bit of that. Enough so that he might be able to buy himself enough time to get out of town if the hired gun came looking for him.

Money spoke a language everyone understood.

He poured himself another shot, added the last bit of Coke from the can, and mixed it with his index finger. He wiped the finger on his jeans, took a sip and stood up, carrying the tumbler with him.

He glanced at the clock on the stove and saw it was close to nine. His wife wouldn't be home until ten, which was when the women's knitting club finished at the Congregationalist Church. He smiled at the thought of her making blankets for the babies up at the NICU in Lebanon and headed for his den.

When he reached the three steps that led down into the den, he paused to take a drink. The lights flickered, and he felt a cold hand on the back of his head.

Before he could say a word, a massive force thrust him forward, launching him into the room. The hand remained on the back of his head and slammed it down onto the corner of the coffee table.

The mahogany edge splintered even as the point of it split Omer's skull from his left temple across the forehead and to the other side.

The world went black, and Omer hit the floor. He felt his body go slack, the tumbler falling from his hand and rattling across the slate that served as the fireplace's surround.

"It's a shame you can't see your own head," a voice remarked. "I can actually see your brains. I suspect you know you're going to die now."

Omer tried to speak, to curse at the stranger in his house, but neither his mouth nor his tongue responded. His heartbeat grew loud in his ears, and he heard the strange, rhythmless thump of it.

"If it's any consolation," the stranger continued, "I don't hate you. Hell, I don't even know you. What's more important, though, is the fact that you're not the only one. You weren't the first, and you won't be the last. I've a few more to take care of."

The stranger said something else, but Omer couldn't understand. The words no longer made sense, and an odd chill enveloped him.

He knew he was dying. He would be dead in a matter of minutes, if not sooner.

He realized that his wife would come home to find his body and the mess that she'd be left with.

At least, he thought, he had said I love you when she had walked out the door.

At least there was that.

✳ ✳ ✳

"Is it done already?" Ezra asked.

Theo nodded, a broad and malicious grin on his face. "It was easy. A hell of a lot easier than the first."

"He's dead?" Ezra kept his voice low, painfully aware that he was in a residential neighborhood and standing near an empty baseball field.

"Yes," Theo answered. "Made sure to watch him stop breathing and everything. It's a bit of a mess, though."

Ezra snorted. "A mess is fine. Did you make this one look like a suicide, too?"

"No," the dead man replied, shaking his head. "He was drinking, so I just helped him split his head open. I thought it was just the first you wanted to have look like a suicide."

"It was," Ezra confirmed. "I was merely curious."

"Well, you don't have to worry about this one." The dead man turned and looked at Omer's house on the other side of the field.

"What is it?" Ezra asked.

"I'm wondering," Theo said. "Do you think that fella who saw me at Kenny's house will come looking for me here?"

"It won't matter if he does," Ezra replied. "You won't be here."

Theo shrugged and waited as Ezra retrieved the button.

CHAPTER 20
GONE

Stan and Adam entered Kenny's house through the back door. Both carried a pair of lead-lined boxes, and Adam appeared uncomfortable. Stan would have to speak with him later, try to soothe some of the younger man's fears.

"You saw someone here?" Adam asked as he closed the door.

"I did," Stan confirmed. "It is my hope he is still here. I suspect he had something to do with the attack on Kenny."

"Why?"

There was a great deal in that question, and Stan answered it as best he could.

"I know Kenny would not commit suicide, and especially not by hanging. In all things, Kenny was considerate," Stan explained. "His suicide would have been no different. There are, I have learned, some issues at the factory. Kenny was a natural leader, and from what he had told me, he was leading people in a quiet revolt. They were not striking, but they were making the extra production difficult."

Adam frowned. "Why?"

"New management demanded longer hours for less pay and less benefits," Stan stated. "Or so I was told."

"That'd do it."

Stan nodded. "I suspect someone wanted to punish Kenny. Perhaps even frighten others into behaving. I cannot know for certain, of course, but this is what I suspect."

"Why would they target him? Just because he was a leader?"

"Precisely why." Stan turned into Kenny's den. "If this were an armed revolt, they might take him prisoner and hold a mock trial, something to bring the others to heel. In this case, violence will be enough to shock the workers into obeying. And if the death of one doesn't suffice, they will move on to the next."

"Next leader?"

Stan nodded and led the way up the stairs to the second floor.

"How soon will they attack someone else?" Adam asked.

Stan shrugged. "I should think they would wait to see how the workers react to Kenny's imminent death. If the workers do as they are told, then there should be no issues. All will be well. If, however, they decide to keep pushing back against the demands made upon them by the new owners, then I suspect the result will be another death. Perhaps more public than Kenny's."

"Another suicide?" Adam opened the door to Kenny's bedroom, and Stan glanced in and turned away from where they had found his friend.

"I suspect it would be another suicide," Stan answered as they searched the rest of the second floor. "For the skilled individual, a suicide is easy to fake. For an assassin who is already dead, I can only imagine that it would be much easier."

They finished searching the house and found nothing. Not a hint of the dead man.

Frowning, Stan thought of the ghost, the way it had leaped out of the house and raced for the rear of the backyard. Perhaps beyond the trees, the dead man's object could be found.

They left the house, and Stan turned to Adam. "Would you feel comfortable searching the woods with me?"

"Yeah," Adam chuckled, nodding. "That's not a problem. What are we looking for in the dark, Stan?"

"I will be looking for a ghost," Stan answered. "I would simply appreciate the company."

Adam laughed, and the two of them crossed the backyard to the tree line.

They searched for the better part of an hour, but Stan saw no sign of a ghost.

Not a single thing.

"Hey," Adam said. "Looks like a little trail over here. Didn't see it before when we came through the other way."

Stan's shoulders sagged. "I had forgotten about this trail. It runs to a pair of side streets on either end."

"So, what does that mean?"

Stan heard the uncertainty in the younger man and remembered there was much more he had to teach Adam about the dead.

"It means that more than likely, someone parked on one of the side streets," Stan explained. "They then walked to a point along the path where they could see Kenny's house and determine if he was at home or not. They then would have left the dead man's object, for Kenny's house is well within the range of a ghost from this spot. Once Kenny was killed, or nearly killed, the ghost would have been retrieved."

"So, the ghost could be anywhere?" Adam asked.

"Yes, unfortunately."

Adam frowned. "What now?"

"Now," Stan sighed, "we return home, and I will see Kenny in the morning. I wish to say my goodbyes to my friend."

"Pretty sure Mack will let me borrow his truck if we're going to Nashua," Adam offered.

"Yes," Stan nodded. "I am sure you are right. Although Sheriff Bowman could drive me there as well."

Stan glanced once more at the trail, then headed back toward Kenny's house.

✳ ✳ ✳

"Do you have a problem with killing a woman?" Ezra asked.

Theo frowned. "I don't know. I've never killed one. Beaten a few here and there, but it wasn't uncalled for. They didn't do as they were told."

"Fair enough, I suppose," Ezra stated. He looked down Lake Street at the small ranch-style house at the intersection of Lake and Olive. "Do you see that lime green house there, at the corner?"

Theo looked and nodded. "There a broad in there you need killed?"

"Indeed, there is. Her name is Annie Hamm. She might be with her husband. She might not," Ezra informed him. "I confess, I don't know many of the particulars of Annie. She has only recently been made a leader of her shift. However, this has not stopped her from being a full and active voice in the intentional slowdown at my factory."

"Do I kill them both?" Theo asked.

Ezra rubbed his chin. "No. Not at all. I can't fault the man for marrying the woman he did. Try and get her alone."

"If I don't kill them both," Theo said, "and I just kill her, they're going to point the finger at him, you know."

"Hmm, yes, I'd thought of that. I haven't quite worked out how to get around it, though."

The two sat in silence on a small bench at a bus stop. Ezra had an earpiece in to give the impression that he was on a phone call and not speaking to himself.

"I have read," Ezra began, "where some ghosts have reached into the chests of their victims and squeezed their hearts."

"Really?" Theo asked, surprised.

Ezra nodded. "Yes. Some have stuck their hands into the skulls of others. I recently discovered some information about the entire process. I think it's something you could do, especially since you're able to manipulate objects."

"Would I stick my hand into the top of her head and, I don't know, kind of mix it around like I was mashing a cake or something?"

Ezra chuckled at the image. "Yes, I suppose that would work quite well. If you decide to do it that way, Theo, there is one favor I would ask."

"What's that?"

"Make sure you remember exactly what you've done," Ezra smiled. "I want to hear all about it when you're finished."

✳ ✳ ✳

Annie put down her crossword puzzle, removed her reading glasses and stared at the floor for a moment. From the bedroom, she heard her husband's snores. He didn't think it was odd that Kenny had tried to commit suicide. Didn't think anything was odd.

But then again, Annie had married Mitch for his looks and not his brains.

She glanced at the glass of flat Pepsi standing on the coffee table among a pile of hunting and fishing magazines and wondered if Mitch would ever learn to put the magazines in the recycling bin when he was done with them. She doubted it.

The mess didn't irritate her as it normally did.

In fact, she found a strange sort of comfort in it.

Mitch's messes, of which there were many, were steadfast and true. She could count on them. Annie knew that when she walked into the bathroom, she would need to straighten his towel. It would, invariably, be lumped up and still damp from his afternoon shower. The toothpaste cap would be off and on the left side of the sink, while the tube itself would be on the right. His underwear, in desperate need of replacement, would be in a jumble by the hamper. Not in it, not even hanging out of it, but directly in front of it as though it were a welcome mat.

The imagery, which normally brought up a sullen rage at Mitch's ineptitude regarding the most basic of self-care tasks, soothed her.

Mitch's messes were a normal, expected part of the day.

Kenny's attempted suicide was not.

Annie realized she shouldn't think of it as an attempted suicide. According to the doctor who had spoken with Sheriff Bowman, Kenny wasn't going to survive.

She glanced at her phone and wondered when Omer was going to text her. He was supposed to give her an update on how things were during his shift at the factory. It would be difficult to get the rest of the workers to tough out the slowdown with Kenny gone, and she needed to know how Omer had fared.

She picked up the phone and considered sending a quick text to see what the hell was going on, but then she let the phone drop to the couch. Omer would get all upset if she bothered him.

"Strange duck," she muttered and got to her feet. She straightened Mitch's magazines, picked up the glass of flat Pepsi, and walked down the hall and into the kitchen. As she stepped across the threshold, Annie paused.

The lights flickered several times and for a split second, she thought she saw someone standing in front of the kitchen sink.

But no one was there.

She shook her head, walked to the sink and dumped out the soda. As she rinsed the glass, the lights flickered again, and she looked up.

Annie saw her reflection in the window and directly behind her, the shape of a man.

Before she could react, something terrible and cold plunged into the back of her head, and a freezing chill spread throughout her body.

She stood limp, knowing the only reason she was upright was due to whatever had been thrust into her skull. Annie hung there, her vision dimming.

"It'll be over in a minute, doll," a man's voice whispered. "Hope it ain't as painful as I think it is."

Annie discovered that it wasn't, and a moment later, she wasn't worried about anything at all.

CHAPTER 21

THE WAITING ROOM

Stan sat in the waiting room of the ICU at Southern New Hampshire Medical Center in Nashua. Sheriff Bowman was speaking with a doctor, and Stan had brought along a book with him. Unfortunately, he found himself unable to concentrate on the words, and so he held the book in his hands, his fingers tracing the gilt lettering on the spine. It was an early edition of Hawthorne's *House of Seven Gables*, and the leather felt good against his skin.

He didn't know why he thought he would be able to read while waiting for Kenny to pass, but some part of him had.

Marilyn had encouraged the bringing of the book, because she knew him better than he knew himself most days. He suspected she understood the tactile sensation of the leather would act as a balm for his nerves.

Marilyn understood more than anyone thought.

The security door between the ICU and the waiting room opened, and Sheriff Bowman stepped out. He held his hat in his hands as he sat down across from Stan.

"They haven't found any relatives," the sheriff began. "Least none that are alive."

Stan nodded.

Sheriff Bowman cleared his throat. "He didn't have a living will either, so the hospital is going to take Kenny off life support in just a little bit, but not until you've said your goodbye."

"Thank you," Stan said.

"Well, you two were close," the sheriff stated. "I know he helped you through a lot when you first came home. Only seems right that you get your say."

Stan looked down at the book in his hand.

"Just let me know when you're ready, Stan."

"I am ready," Stan replied, looking back up and at the sheriff.

Sheriff Bowman nodded, got to his feet and went to the door. Stan followed, and the security door opened a moment later. A short, slight nurse of indeterminate age guided them around to the left of the ICU and brought them to a room. Without a word, she left them, and when Stan stepped to the opening to enter, he glanced at the sheriff.

Sheriff Bowman shook his head. "Go on in, Stan. I've said my goodbyes alone. You should do the same."

Stan walked into the room and saw his friend.

Kenny, despite his size, looked small in the hospital bed. He was diminished by the tubes and the wires that clung to him and entered his flesh. Machines whirred, and soft sounds filled the room. The stringent stench of chemicals hung in the air, and Stan found himself painfully reminded of Walter Reed Hospital and the long, slow treatments of his wounds.

Unlike Stan, Kenny would not wake up. He would not rise from the hospital bed and find he could see the dead.

The thought that Kenny might not leave the earth, that he might, in fact, remain behind, burned through Stan.

It was a fate he did not want his friend to suffer.

Stan saw how many of the dead viewed their continued existence as some form of punishment that they had somehow failed to live up to their own religious obligations. He knew it couldn't be further from the truth. No one, as far as he could ascertain, knew why some of the dead remained and others did not.

Good or bad or indifferent. None of it made any difference when it came to staying behind.

Stan looked down at Kenny.

"It is said by some that those in comas can hear what we say," Stan began. "If you can hear me, Kenny, know that I am your friend. Know that you did more for me than anyone else in my life, and I wish I could do more for you."

Stan waited a moment longer, then turned and left the room.

The time for mourning had passed.

Stan drifted off to sleep on the ride from the hospital back to Mason, and memories of his past swarmed up from the depths of his subconscious.

He found himself not in the front seat of Sheriff Bowman's patrol vehicle but sitting on his hospital bed in Walter Reed. The curtain was drawn, and the door was closed. The room remained in darkness, and it was long after visiting hours.

Yet no one had visited Stan. He didn't mind.

He liked the solitude.

In his dream, he could remember his anger. The rage that infected every thought and action. Some of it came from the wounds he had suffered, the pain and the outrage at having been wounded. Most of it came from the hatred he harbored for his own family. The misery they had put him through as a child and teen, the push for him to leave the house and seek his fortune elsewhere, anywhere other than Mason, New Hampshire.

The Army had offered him the quickest shipping date to basic training.

The quickest ticket out of New Hampshire.

Stan hadn't written home, despite being forced to write by the drill sergeants. He had, instead, written to the few friends he had in high school.

None of them were still alive.

Yet those deaths hadn't occurred, not before his wounding or even during his time in the hospital. Those deaths had come afterward, in the first few years after returning to Mason.

And had his family not died while he was away, he wouldn't have returned to New Hampshire at all.

His dream shifted from these memories back to the hospital room, and he heard a pair of nurses talking about the marriage of a third.

In his dream, Stan shivered.

He knew this memory. He knew what was coming next.

And a heartbeat later, it arrived.

A man drifted through the left wall of Stan's room and came to a stop a few feet from him. The man's arms and legs were gone, as were his eyes. His mouth, though raw and injured, was still there, as were both of his ears. He hung, suspended, directly before the door, then rotated to face Stan.

A long, low groan escaped the dead man's mouth, and Stan couldn't tell if he was hallucinating or not. Perhaps they had given him a new medication, or maybe a piece of iron had traveled along with the blood into his brain, and he was having a stroke.

Stan continued to stare at the ghost, and the ghost drifted back.

"You can see me."

The ghost's voice was low and hoarse, the surprise in it mirroring Stan's own.

The dead man drifted closer, and Stan screamed.

✳ ✳ ✳

Stan sat upright in the cruiser as Sheriff Bowman pulled the vehicle into a parking space at the station.

"You okay?"

Stan nodded. "A bit of a bad dream, Sheriff, nothing more."

Sheriff Bowman glanced over at him. "Doesn't sound like a bit of a bad dream. Sounded like it was horrifying."

Stan offered him a small smile. "Perhaps another time I will tell you of my dreams."

"Not sure I want to hear about them," the sheriff stated as he turned off the vehicle.

They exited at the same time, the closing of their doors ringing out as one against the brick face of the station.

"You want a ride home after I check in?" Sheriff Bowman asked, holding the door open for Stan.

"Thank you, but no," Stan answered. "I will walk home. Perhaps I will visit Mack. I am not certain yet."

They passed through the foyer, and as they headed for the offices, Virgil Cummings came out from the back.

"Don't get too comfortable, Sheriff," the young deputy said.

As the sheriff came to a stop, so too did Stan.

"What's going on?"

"We've got two deaths," Virgil replied, his eyes flicking to Stan for a moment.

Sheriff Bowman shook his head. "He's fine, Virgil. Tell me what happened."

"Looks like Omer had a couple of drinks too many last night," the young deputy explained. "His wife got home late and went right to bed. She thought Omer was asleep in their den. She never checked on him since she'd had a couple of drinks, too. Turns out he fell in their den and split his skull open."

"And the other?" Sheriff Bowman asked.

"Annie Hamm," Virgil said. "They're not sure what happened yet.

Mitch said she just keeled right over in the kitchen. Coroner thinks she might have had an aneurysm or something."

Sheriff Bowman muttered and cursed under his breath. "We got people at both?"

Virgil nodded. "Analise is covering Annie's. I called in Bert Dupont and he's over at Omer's. I knew you were at the hospital and didn't want to bother you."

"I appreciate that," the sheriff sighed. "Bert won't mind being called in. Anything to supplement his pension."

Sheriff Bowman turned to Stan. "Seems like I'm going past Marilyn's. You sure you don't want a ride? At least to Mack's?"

"I am quite sure, Sheriff," Stan assured him. "I will leave you to your work, gentlemen."

Without another word, Stan turned and left the station. He passed by the Sheriff's vehicle and listened to the engine pop and creak as it cooled. The faint odor of hot oil wafted up from the hood, and the scent brought with it unwanted memories of Iraq and the highway of death.

Stan stumbled half a step but righted himself immediately. He had no desire to fall and be in the middle of picking himself up when the sheriff exited the building, which the man was sure to do at any moment. There were two dead, after all.

Stan frowned and considered that information as he walked toward Mack's.

Kenny was dead.

Annie was dead.

Omer was dead.

All three had worked at the factory, which wasn't unusual. Most folks in Mason and the outlying towns did. But what was unusual was the fact that all three had been leaders on their shifts, Kenny more so. The men and women of the factory looked to Kenny for guidance, and it was his steady hand that had brought them to the decision to slow down production. Not too much, but enough to make a point that the new owner and management couldn't interfere with a worker's private life.

A ghost had been the cause of Kenny's death. Of that, Stan was certain.

And now, Omer was dead. Yes, the man had drunk quite a bit, but Stan didn't think he would die in such a way. Although there was always the chance. It was the same with Annie. No one knew when something like an aneurysm would strike, but it was a curious coincidence.

Stan had no doubt that a ghost could have killed Annie and Omer.

He knew, better than most, what the dead could do.

CHAPTER 22
PRECAUTIONS

Ezra enjoyed working with Theo, and while the other two ghosts had yet to make themselves known, Ezra wanted to work with more.

He sat down at a small desk, jotted down some notes regarding the experience of interacting with Theo, and then closed his notebook. He ran his fingers through his hair, took a glass of water, and then picked up his phone. He dialed the number for the same shop he had purchased the others from and waited.

The call went through, and when it was answered, they didn't ask who it was.

"Good evening, sir," the familiar voice greeted. "I trust all is well?"

"Yes," Ezra replied. "The first item is working out phenomenally. The other two have not made themselves known yet."

Ezra listened to the heavy pause, knowing that the man on the other end was worried there might be some questions about a possible refund.

"I know they'll come out soon enough," Ezra continued. "I would, however, like to have a few more sent to me if at all possible."

Ezra heard the man's sigh of relief and then a genuine chuckle. "Of course, sir. And considering the previous two have decided to play coy, I am certain we can knock off a bit of the price for you if that interests you."

Ezra laughed and relaxed in his chair. "Discounts always interest me. I'm looking for three or four more. They don't need to have a history of violence, but they should be comfortable with it if at all possible."

"Oh, I'm sure we can find something in the warehouse," the seller responded. "Do you need them quickly? We would be willing to cover the cost of overnighting as well if that was something you required, sir."

"The quicker, the better," Ezra admitted. "I am, unfortunately, pressed for time at this moment. Recalcitrant workers and the such."

"Ah, I understand completely, sir. I'll overnight a trio of, let us say, well, aggressive stock."

"That would be fantastic," Ezra informed the man.

And with that, the two of them went about the business of settling on a price.

With his belly full, Stan walked along Main Street away from Marilyn's house, leaving both Mack's and home behind him. He needed to think, and while Marilyn would leave him alone, Adam was still learning that Stan required time to himself.

Keeping his head down, he let his feet guide him, unconcerned with where he might end up. He knew his town, and he knew it well. There was not a street, bike path, or backyard trail he did not know, and if there was a new one, he could find it easily enough.

There were plenty of dead in town who were willing to speak with him.

He considered reaching out to them concerning the attack on Kenny but decided it would be a poor course of action. Whatever ghost had attacked Kenny had done so quickly, and there weren't any ghosts directly around Kenny's home.

The deaths of the two other workers bothered Stan as well. He did not wish to bring his suspicions to the sheriff, not without any evidence, and even then, he wasn't quite certain what he would be able to do about it. How could the sheriff speak to someone about fatal accidents or organ failure and accuse them of using ghosts to kill the victims?

No, it was a non-starter, as Adam had a habit of saying.

Stan would need to investigate the deaths, and more than likely, he would need to bring Adam into the examination of the incidents as well.

And Stan wasn't quite certain the young man was up to the task.

Adam was bright and courageous enough, but before the winter, the young man had suffered a terrible scare. One that had struck deep and left him with a fear of the dead.

The younger man was working through his newfound trepidation, and Stan was helping him with it. But there was a stark difference between speaking with a dead man in the cemetery and hunting down an unknown individual, killing local citizens.

Stan took a deep breath, came to a stop and lifted his head.

He blinked, looked around, and saw he was standing in front of the driveway to his family's home. For some reason he couldn't quite understand, he wasn't surprised.

He hesitated for a moment, then walked up the long drive to the final barrier. Clasping his hands behind his back, Stan cleared his throat and waited.

Philomena came out of the house, floating across the ground with a dramatic flair that seemed embedded in her personality. She came to a stop a short distance from him on the other side of the salt line. She raised an imperious eyebrow and asked, "What has sent you here again, Stanley?"

Stan opened his mouth to say he didn't know, but instead, he answered, "I have a question."

"You have a question for me?" His dead aunt shook her head and let out a long, hard laugh. "This is not something I ever thought would happen. Tell me, nephew, what could you possibly need to ask me?"

"How do I destroy the dead with something other than fire?"

She glided back a short distance, her hands clenched into fists. "You come here and threaten me?!"

Stan frowned, realized how it must have sounded, and shook his head.

"No, Aunt, I have misspoken," he explained. "I come asking about a ghost in town. One who, I am reasonably certain, is not a native of Mason."

"You want to destroy a different ghost?" she asked for clarification.

Stan nodded.

"And a ghost that is not a native, too?" Philomena drifted closer.

"Yes."

"What has this ghost done?" Philomena asked.

"Killed my friend, Kenny."

"Kenny?" She laughed, then the laugh stopped. "Kenneth Langsam? Meredith Langsam's son?"

"Yes."

Philomena straightened up, her expression one of fury. "Kenneth Langsam was my godson."

Stan did not bother to hide his surprised expression.

The dead woman gave a short nod. "He and his mother were two of the few people I liked in this miserable town, and when cancer took her, and he left for the war, there was no one left worth a thing."

Stan remained silent.

"And someone has killed my godson," she muttered, shaking her head. After a moment, she straightened up, regained her composure and looked at Stan.

"Destroying a ghost can be easy," Philomena told him. "Although it is not without its dangers. These dangers come not only from the ghost itself but also from the person who has control of the object the dead are attached to. This person can cause far more damage than you think. But I digress. I could have gone the rest of your life without you knowing what I will tell you next, nephew, but I am willing to risk it for my godson."

She looked at Stan and then muttered something he couldn't quite make out.

"Let us say your ghost has attached himself to a bit of his own bone," Philomena began. "For you, your initial instinct is to burn the bone. This would take far too long, even should you douse it in kerosene. There are other ways, though. A hammer, for instance, would shatter the bone. Should you smash it, the bone will explode. If the ghost is strong, you will suffer. If it is not, you'll still suffer, just not as much. Do you understand me?"

"I think I do," Stan answered. "I can break the item in order to destroy the ghost."

"Yes."

Stan looked at his dead great-aunt and wondered what had gone wrong in her life that had made her so miserable. He remembered her beating and howling at him when he was a child and in her care.

"I am sorry Kenneth passed," Philomena stated, interrupting Stan's thoughts. "I hope he has gone on to his just reward and that he is not trapped here. Offer up a prayer for me, Stanley Owens, and let me know when you destroy Kenneth's killer."

The dead woman turned and walked away, vanishing back into the house.

Stan remained where he was, feeling odd and trying to put his finger on why.

It came to him a heartbeat later.

Philomena had not cursed him out as she walked away. Nor had she threatened him.

She had well and truly just walked away.

She trusted him to kill the killer, and Stan felt an odd sense of gratitude and pride in that.

CHAPTER 23

STORIES TOLD

"Are you okay?"

"Hmm?" Stan looked up and found Adam standing in the doorway to his room. Glancing around, Stan saw he had started to remove his shoes earlier, but only one was off. His cufflinks were on the small chest of drawers, as were his wallet and watch. On his bed table stood his windup clock, and it ticked off the seconds toward ten o'clock at night.

"Are you okay?" Adam repeated.

Stan considered the question, then shook his head. "No. I don't think I am. In fact, I think I may be suffering from paranoia."

Adam folded his arms across his chest, leaned in the doorway and asked, "How do you figure that?"

"You know my friend Kenny passed away today?"

Adam nodded.

"Two of his coworkers have passed away in the last two days as well."

"That's terrible," Adam remarked. "I'm sorry to hear that."

"As am I."

"What's making you paranoid? The fact that three people are dead so close together?"

"More than that," Stan replied. "It's the timing of it all. I saw the ghost in Kenny's house. My fear is that the other deaths occurred because the same ghost killed them."

Adam's eyes widened. "Is that what's being said? That ghosts killed them?"

"No," Stan answered, shaking his head. "Not at all. It is merely my own suspicion. There is no evidence. Omer L'Étrange enjoyed drinking a little too much at times. An accident is not too far-fetched. And as for Annie Hamm, well, they won't know what killed her until they perform an autopsy, and that's only if the authorities feel it necessary to do so."

"Is there anything we should do?" Adam asked. "Places we should look, something like that?"

"No," Stan told him. "I will keep my eyes open, but there is little else we can do, I am afraid."

They were silent for a moment, then Adam asked, "When was the first time you ever saw a ghost?"

"That is an interesting question," Stan replied after a moment. "Perhaps we should discuss this in the front parlor. It will be far more comfortable."

"Sure."

Stan stood, and the two of them made their way to the first floor, turned on the lights in the parlor, and each took a seat. Adam adjusted his slightly so he might be able to look better at Stan.

"I saw ghosts from time to time as a child," Stan began. "Nothing profound, mind you. Just the typical sightings most children have. None of them particularly bothered me, either. I don't think I quite believed what I was seeing. I think, to be honest, I was imagining them. Perhaps I was. But the first real ghost I saw and knew to be a ghost and not a figment of my imagination was when I was at Walter Reed Hospital."

"What were you at Walter Reed for?"

Stan smiled tiredly. "I was wounded in Iraq. My wounds were fairly severe, and so I was sent back Stateside and then worked on at Walter Reed."

Adam appeared confused.

"Do you know what an IED is? An improvised explosive device?" Stan asked.

"Sure," Adam nodded. "You hear about them in the news all the time."

"That's essentially what I stumbled upon. I was helping along the highway of death in Iraq, and I triggered an IED. It was of far rougher construction than what the troops are facing now. I was fortunate in that it only filled me with iron."

"Wait. What?"

"Iron," Stan repeated. "Several explosive experts talked with me while I was at Walter Reed. Whoever had built the IED had wrapped the explosive portion in pieces of iron. Hundreds of them. The goal of the device was to shred whoever triggered it. Either I am one of the luckiest people alive, or the bomb makers failed miserably at their jobs. Regardless to why, the IED wasn't as powerful as the explosive experts suspected it should have been. With the amount of iron lodged in my body, they felt the bomb-maker's goal had been to shred the target."

"Were they able to get all of the steel out?" Adam asked.

Stan shook his head. "Not steel, iron. And no. I have quite a bit inside of me."

"Does the iron have something to do with seeing ghosts now?"

"No," Stan answered. "While I do not have a formal answer of any sort, I do believe that the explosion triggered something in my brain. It either broke a connection or perhaps opened a connection, I'm not sure which. Either way, Adam, a short time after my injury, I was able to see people who weren't there."

"That must have been terrible," Adam muttered. "Did you think you were going crazy?"

"At first," Stan acknowledged. "And I probably would have thought I was crazy, but then I met an older man who worked at the hospital. He was a volunteer, and he could see the dead."

CHAPTER 24

TRAINING

The dead had been overnighted, exactly as promised.

The small boxes stood on the table, the table itself surrounded by a ring of salt. Each box stood open, revealing the precious cargo inside. One held a yellowed human tooth with a cracked steel filling, another a gold ring with a broken setting, and the third contained a lock of blonde hair.

Ezra looked down at the note he was holding.

> *The tooth belongs to Darryl Rarest, the gold ring to Hyacinth Gage, and the lock of blonde hair to Lars Olafson. Unlike your recalcitrant purchases, these three are rather ambitious in their own ways.*

Ezra took a deep breath and said, "My name is Ezra, and I am asking for the three of you to exit your objects and speak with me."

The temperature in the room plummeted.

An involuntary shiver raced through him, and Ezra clenched his teeth and squeezed his hands into fists, silently cursing himself for forgetting to put on warm clothing.

One by one, though, the dead appeared.

A small woman, no taller than five feet, formed first. She wore a plain, dark blue house dress and her hair was pulled back into a messy bun. A very large blood stain filled the center of the dress, and her pale face fixed upon him.

Ezra ignored the dead woman's stare and watched as a pair of men appeared on either side of her. The man on her left was only a few inches taller, and his hair was as blonde as that in the box. But even from where Ezra stood, he could tell the man's hair was dyed. The second man stood on her right, and he was well over six feet, a hulking giant of a man with broad shoulders and an almost square head. Ezra could not see how the shorter man had died, but the giant man had a pair of bullet holes in the side of his head.

There were no exit wounds, and for that, Ezra was thankful.

"Who are you?" the shorter man, Darryl, asked.

"I'm Ezra," he stated. "I have purchased you."

"What for?" Darryl demanded, and Ezra wondered if the dead man had already established himself as the leader among the dead.

Before Ezra could answer the short man's question, the giant, Lars, reached over, took hold of the short man and hauled him up by the nape of his neck.

"No one asked you to ask questions," the giant snarled. "Why don't you just shut it and let the guy talk?"

Lars gave Darryl a shake and then dropped him down. The shorter ghost sneered at the larger one but remained silent.

The dead woman, Hyacinth, stepped closer to Lars.

Ezra nodded his appreciation.

"I have been told," Ezra continued, "that the three of you are not averse to a little violence. I am in need of violence, just not killing. Not yet, at least. However, I will need you to keep some of my employees in line."

The small ghost snorted, scratched at the side of his nose and asked, "How much violence we talkin' about?"

Lars nodded his agreement. "Yes. How much?"

"I'm not quite certain, yet," Ezra confessed. "However, it will need to be a sufficient enough amount to ensure proper behavior on the part of my workers."

"I don't care about the amount of violence," Hyacinth said, her voice soft and delicate. "I care about the amount of pain I can inflict."

"I need them alive," Ezra told them. "Dead workers cannot work. Workers in the hospital cannot work. We must, I am sorry to say, be moderate."

Hyacinth looked at him with disdain but said nothing more.

"Are we agreed, then?" Ezra asked, looking at the others.

Lars and Darryl nodded with glum expressions.

"Theo?" Ezra asked.

The dead sailor stepped into the room and looked at his new colleagues.

"This is Theo," Ezra stated. "He and I have been working together for a short time, but it is a time long enough for him to know what it is that I want. He will speak to you about this, and I will decide what individuals you should focus on."

Ezra nodded to Theo, collected his wallet and keys, and left the suite. Once, he stood in the hallway, and as the door clicked shut behind him, he shivered.

The temperature in his rented rooms had been far below what he found to be comfortable. He would have to either invest in warmer clothing or turn up the heat.

Increasing the heat, though, might lead to unnecessary questions from the hotel's management. And while money tended to answer most questions, Ezra didn't want to interact with any more people than was absolutely necessary.

With that thought at the forefront, he walked toward the elevators. He had a meeting with James. One, he hoped, that would prove to be positive.

✳ ✳ ✳

"They're scared, sir," James stated.

Ezra watched as his employee's hand shook before it took hold of the glass of beer. "What else is happening, James?"

James wet his lips, took a long drink, cleared his throat and muttered, "They're scared, but some of them are still making noise about slowing down. Not as much as the others wanted, but a little bit. 'In honor of Kenny,' one of them said."

Ezra raised an eyebrow and took a sip of wine.

James smiled nervously.

"Who said it?" Ezra asked.

James fumbled as he took a small, dark green moleskin notebook out of his pocket. He flipped through several pages then found what he was looking for.

"That would be Finn Reddington," James answered. "First shift machinist."

"Skilled?"

"Very much so, sir."

Ezra sighed. "Does he have much to do now?"

"Basic repairs," James stated. "However, he mostly oversees his apprentice."

"Does he?"

James nodded.

"In theory, he could do that from a chair, if needed, correct?" Ezra asked.

"Probably, sir."

"Excellent. Do me a favor. When you return to the office, see what his schedule is like this week and then send me the information. His home address as well. Understood?" Ezra finished his wine.

"Quite, sir," James answered. "I'm—I'm not going to have to do anything, am I?"

"No," Ezra reassured him. "I have something else entirely planned for Mr. Reddington."

CHAPTER 25
MEMORIES, WALTER REED HOSPITAL

Stan sat in his room, too afraid to leave. Sweat dried on his skin, and his body ached. He'd fought hard against the orderlies and refused to exit his room for any reason.

They had asked him why, and he had remained silent.

Stan kept his back to the window, his eyes locked on the door, all the lights on in the room.

A soft knock broke the silence, and before he could answer, the doorknob turned, and a stranger entered the room. Unlike the others, this man didn't wear an orderly's uniform, nor did he wear the coat of a doctor.

He wore, instead, a battered Carhartt jacket, denim jeans that had long since seen better days, and a pair of well-cared-for combat boots. The man's steel-colored hair was clipped short to his head, and the stranger's tanned skin appeared to have a thousand cracks in it. The stranger stood well under six feet, and the smile on his face was genuine. Beyond the man, Stan saw members of the hospital staff, all watching.

"Do you mind if I close the door, Stan?" the stranger asked.

Stan shook his head.

The stranger closed the door, sat down in the room's other chair and folded large, arthritic hands onto his lap.

"My name's Elwood," the stranger said by way of introduction. "I know you don't know me and that I sure as hell don't look like a shrink. Or any other member of the medical trade. You'd be right about that. And I suppose you're wondering why I'm in here."

Stan nodded.

"Well, I worked in this building for decades," Elwood explained. "Shortly after I got out of the Army in 1946. I know this building better than anyone alive, and I don't say that with pride. It's a matter of fact and nothing more. I retired a few years ago, and that was mostly to be with my dog, who was on his way out, as they say. Before I retired and after, they would call me when someone acted like you had."

Stan licked his lips and remained silent, unsure as to where the conversation was going.

"Back in the day, they would have said you'd lost your mind," Elwood stated. "Said you'd gone off the deep end and needed to be sent to a place with padded rooms. You and I know that's not true, although you might not know it yet. No, see, when I get called in, Stan, it's because someone saw a ghost."

Stan stiffened, and Elwood nodded.

"Yes, there's no hiding it," the older man said. "Not quite like the movies where everyone just runs amok and starts shouting about it. Sometimes, the first one you see is absolutely terrifying, and that can set the tone for the rest of your life."

Stan cleared his throat, glanced at the door and then back to Elwood before asking in a low voice, "You have seen the dead yourself?"

"Many times," Elwood confessed, keeping his own voice low. "But I saw them long before I joined the Army and went overseas. A few have been like me, but for most, recovering from an injury tends to be the first time they witness ghosts. That's what happened to you."

Stan knew it wasn't a question but a statement.

"Last night," Stan explained. "A man came into the room through the wall."

"What did he look like?"

Stan swallowed hard and answered, "He was missing all his limbs and his eyes. But even so, he knew I was there. He knew I could see him."

"Ah," Elwood sighed. "That would be Corporal Aaron Llewelyn. He is a good enough fellow, but his appearance is terrifying. I am sorry he was the first you saw. I suspect he spoke to you?"

Stan nodded. "He was surprised I could see him. Then, he drifted closer, and I… I started screaming."

"A sane reaction," Elwood reassured him. "I trust the good corporal vanished a moment later?"

"He did," Stan confirmed. "He sank through the floor. But I couldn't stop screaming. They gave me a shot, but when I woke up this morning, the ghost… corporal, he was back and looking toward me. He heard me inhale to scream, and he took off again."

"And that's when everything started on this wing? Your refusal to leave the room?" Elwood asked.

Stan nodded.

"That's miserable," Elwood muttered. "Well, the first thing we'll do is straighten this mess out with the head nurse. Her name's Babs, and she's a damned fine nurse. Her mother worked here, too. But that's beside the point. I'll talk to Babs and tell her what's going on, and then you and I will have a chat about it, too."

"What are we going to talk about?" Stan asked as Elwood stood up.

"We're going to talk about ways to keep them away from you and what will ensure your privacy. As for right now, Stan, sit and do your best to relax. I will open the door now so you can tell where everyone is at. Also, it will assure them you are well. Does that sound fair?"

Stan hesitated, then answered, "It does."

"Good," Elwood smiled and opened the door. "This will only take a few minutes."

Stan watched the older man walk out, and the nurses and orderlies congregated around him.

Elwood was, he realized, a well-respected individual in the hospital, and Stan felt a flurry of hope. He watched as Elwood spoke with several individuals, then focused on an older woman, who frowned and shook her head.

Elwood gave the older woman a hug and then returned to the room.

"Of the many dead here, Stan," Elwood began, sitting down once more, "very, very few of them are violent. Most of those who are here are lost. They still don't know their wars have ended. They don't know. Now, regardless as to whether they are lost or are well aware of their situation, you need to know how to keep them out of your room."

"Yes," Stan agreed.

"First, we'll get you some of those cloth draft stoppers," Elwood told him. "We'll fill them with rock salt and line them up around the edge of the room and the windowsill. The salt acts as a block against the dead. They cannot cross it. I can't tell you why, only that they can't."

"That's it?" Stan asked, confused. "I mean, are you sure?"

"I am," Elwood nodded. "That is the easiest. Perhaps the finest one for someone who doesn't want to interact with the dead. If you have the ability, or the desire, rather, you can speak to them."

Stan was about to say he couldn't and then realized he could. He had heard the corporal. Had Stan wished, he could have spoken to him. He knew it as fact.

"What would I say to them?"

Elwood smiled. "You can tell them how uncomfortable you are when they're in your room. They'll stay out of it. Babs will put out the word, too."

"That's it?" Stan asked.

"That's it."

A sense of relief washed over Stan, and he sank in his chair. His wounds ached, and his head throbbed, but the relief was undeniable and welcomed.

"I'll warn you, though, Stan, some of the dead will want to speak with you," Elwood said, and the sense of relief vanished.

"What? Why?" Stan's heart thudded in his chest.

"How often do you think they get to speak with someone new?" Elwood asked in response. "How often can they ask someone about what's going on in the world around them?"

Stan looked out into the crowd of nurses, orderlies and doctors gathered at the nurse's station. Behind them, he saw a man who was dead. Stan could see through the ghost's head, not from any wound but simply because the man's form was almost transparent. There was an eagerness in the dead man's expression.

And Stan understood it perfectly.

"They need to talk," he whispered.

Elwood nodded, glanced out the door and turned back to Stan.

"That's Monty," Elwood informed him. "He died during Vietnam. A nice, quiet fellow. Someone caught up in the times. He died of typhoid fever. He loves the movies."

Stan sighed.

All these dead wanted was to talk.

CHAPTER 26
SETTING SIGHTS

"James," Ezra said.

On the other end of the line, James cleared his throat. "Yes, sir?"

"I'm going to ask you one more time. Are you sure about this?"

Ezra listened to the heavy silence and could imagine James' thoughts churning in his head.

"Yes," James answered a moment later. "I'm certain. Finn Reddington is the one who needs to be corrected."

"All right," Ezra decided, hiding the pleasure he felt. Unbeknownst to James, each call was recorded. Paper trails had been laid out. Alibis were created and destroyed. While no one would believe a ghost killed or harmed anyone in Mason, they would certainly believe that James, a new manager with troublesome employees, brought outside muscle in to solve his problems.

Ezra was nothing if not careful.

"Excellent. I'll get on that immediately."

James mumbled a goodbye and ended the call before Ezra could, and that was fine as far as he was concerned. It was merely more fuel for the fire, should James need to burn.

Ezra returned his phone to the small Faraday bag in his pocket. The bags had proven perfect for protecting the batteries from being drained by the dead. It was a tidbit of information he had learned on a website run by a local couple in New Hampshire. Had he not been so occupied with the factory and its demands, Ezra would have liked to have stopped in and picked their brains. Brian and Jenny Roy seemed, from their website, approachable.

And Ezra always enjoyed extra information.

He put those thoughts away as he removed Hyacinth Gage's gold ring and squatted down in the tree line across from his factory's parking lot. From where he was, Ezra could see the North Entrance, Finn Reddington's preferred ingress and egress from the building. Finn was a man with a bright red shock of hair and pale, freckled skin. He was the only man on this shift with red hair and the only one with a large spider tattooed on the left side of his neck.

"Hyacinth," Ezra whispered as he placed the gold ring on the ground.

She appeared a moment later, a look of curiosity on her face.

"Is that it?" she asked and nodded toward the factory.

"It is."

Hyacinth sniffed, wiped her nose with the back of her hand and asked, "Who is it you want then?"

"A man named Finn Reddington," Ezra answered. "Red-headed man with a spider tattooed on the left side of his neck."

She raised an eyebrow. "What's that?"

"A spider," Ezra repeated. "A tattoo of a spider."

"Why in the name of all that's holy would he be puttin' a thing like that on his neck for?" the dead woman shook her head with genuine confusion. "Was he a sailor? Is that why he did it, then?"

"I don't know," Ezra told her. "Some people like tattoos."

She sniffed, wiped her nose again with the back of her hand and then shrugged. "Well, to each his own, I suppose. What would you like me to do, then?"

Ezra found himself hating the word "then". He smiled at her. "Can you interfere with him and not be seen?"

She grinned and nodded. "Sure enough."

"Can you speak to him without being seen?"

Hyacinth snorted. "Easy."

"Good. Hurt him, and when he falls, tell him to stay in line."

"I'll do it and be back in a jiff." The dead woman gave him an exaggerated wink and then vanished from sight.

Ezra sat down on the ground and waited to see what, if anything, the dead woman could do.

✳ ✳ ✳

Finn Reddington stood up, pulled his pants back into place, adjusted his belt, zipped his fly closed and flushed the toilet. He took his phone off the toilet paper holder, slipped it into his back pocket and let himself out of the stall. He came to a stop in front of the sinks and set about washing his hands, whistling as he cleaned himself, an old habit rather than something done out of pleasure.

Because there was little to be pleased about.

Kenny had died, as had Annie and Omer. There'd be a shake-up soon enough on each shift; people would have to move up into the different shift leader slots. Finn had wanted to be a shift leader, but only when one of the others had retired. He didn't want the job because someone was dead.

He'd take it, of course. Finn needed the money, what with Rita being pregnant and clamoring for a house instead of the duplex they rented.

He shook his head, turned away from the sink and pulled a couple of paper towels out of the dispenser. He dried his hands, and as he did so, the overhead lights flickered.

Frowning, Finn looked up and wondered, not for the first time, if the wiring was finally going to let go. The factory had needed a good going over before it had been sold, and things hadn't gotten any better with the new owners.

They had, now that he thought about it, gotten worse.

136

The new owner, who spoke through the simpering idiot James, seemed intent on running the factory into the ground. A few years earlier, Finn wouldn't have cared.

But now he did. He wanted his raise. He wanted to take care of Rita and whatever kids they happened to have together.

The lights flickered again, and Finn looked up once more at the overhead fluorescents.

When he did, something struck him in the lower back. It felt like a small ball of ice had slammed into his kidney, the pain of it driving the air from his lungs and sending him to his knees. A second punch caught him in the back of the head and sent explosions of light across his eyes. Finn tried to look around and saw nothing. Not a single person in the room with him.

He let his head hang for a moment, the world swimming around him. He closed his eyes, reached out and fumbled around for the countertop. Holding onto it, he took several breaths, raised his head and opened his eyes.

A cold hand wrapped around the back of his neck, the fingers painful against his flesh. Staring into the mirror, he saw nothing.

The hand squeezed tighter, and a voice spoke in his ear.

"Look at you then, with your shock of red hair," a woman hissed. "You're an Irish if I ever saw one, and that's the truth. Have you the wisdom of your people, then, Finn Reddington?"

Finn couldn't answer, his mind frozen with fear.

"Ah, seems as you do. Fair enough. Now, listen well, child of man, this is your warning. Do as you're told, and do it when you're told, all right, then?"

"Yes," Finn managed, his voice hoarse.

"If'n you don't, Finn Reddington, I'll come along and see if your blood's as red as your hair."

The hand vanished from the back of his neck, and Finn let out a shuddering gasp.

He remained on his knees as the lights returned to full strength, and it was a long time before he managed to pull himself into a standing position. When he did, he twisted his head to one side and saw his reflection in the mirror.

A small handprint, red and harsh, stood out on the pale skin of his neck.

Whatever had just happened was real.

Painfully so.

With shaking hands, Finn turned the collar of his flannel shirt up and walked stiffly out of the bathroom.

There was a quota to meet.

No, he realized as the door closed behind him, there was a quota to exceed.

He had no desire for another visit by the unseen woman.

CHAPTER 27

THE FACTORY

"It was frostbite," Sheriff Bowman stated.

Stan set down his teacup, and Adam frowned.

"How does someone get frostbite in the toilet?" Adam asked.

"Got me," the sheriff answered. "But that's what Doc said it was. Damned thing was in the shape of a hand, though."

Sheriff Bowman shifted his attention to Stan. "Any idea as to what might cause that?"

"Yes," Stan answered. "A ghost."

Neither the sheriff nor Adam laughed. Not even a smile broke their grim visages.

"When a ghost touches you, its touch is cold," Stan explained. "The more powerful the entity, the colder the touch. The longer it stays in contact with you, the greater the severity of the frostbite. When did this happen?"

"Yesterday," Sheriff Bowman replied.

"And you could still see the handprint?" Adam asked.

"Just as if someone had slapped their hand in red paint and grabbed the back of his neck," the sheriff stated.

"Who was it, if I may ask?" Stan inquired.

"Finn Reddington," Sheriff Bowman said. He shook his head. "Finn's not one to flights of fancy, and if I hadn't seen the mark myself, I don't know that I would have believed it. Still, I saw it, and he's as solid as they come. Just like the rest of his family."

Stan nodded his agreement. He had known Eamon Reddington,

Finn's father. Neither of them were known to suffer from an extravagance of imagination.

"Was there anything else?" Adam asked.

Sheriff Bowman cleared his throat, dug out a small notebook from his hip pocket and consulted it. "There it is. Thanks, Adam. Yes, it appears the ghost threatened him, too."

"Threatened?" Stan frowned. "How so?"

"Nothing specific," the sheriff said. "Just that the threat was implied. Do your job or else."

"She said that?" Adam inquired.

"Not in those words. Bit more, actually," Sheriff Bowman said. "But that's the gist of it. Get your work done, and keep your head down. Good advice in general, but a little suspicious now that Kenny's dead."

"Where did this happen?" Stan asked.

"At the factory," the sheriff answered.

Stan's frown deepened. "There aren't any ghosts at the factory. There haven't been any. Not ever."

Sheriff Bowman shrugged. "Be that as it may, Stan, that's where Finn said it happened. I talked to a couple of others at the factory, not that Finn knows, but they all say he was different after he made his mid-afternoon trip to the bathroom. He came out looking like someone had shaken him from head to toe, and he had his collar up around his neck. Said he was cold and not feeling well when they asked him about it."

Stan thought of the ghost he had seen at Kenny's house.

He thought of Annie and Omer, too.

There had been a ghost at Kenny's, and if a ghost was responsible for the deaths of Omer and Annie, too, it would make sense that a ghost could be at the factory.

If there was any sense to be made.

Stan stood up, and both the sheriff and Adam looked at him in surprise.

"I am going for a walk," he explained to them. "I will see you soon. Thank you for the information, Sheriff. Adam, will you be seeing Agatha this evening?"

The young man blushed and asked, "How'd you know?"

The sheriff chuckled and answered for Stan. "Adam, you'd be a damned fool not to take a date with Agatha. She's a pretty woman and sharp as a tack. You go on and have a good time, I'll keep an ear out for Stan."

Stan saw that the sheriff, not surprisingly, had handled the situation far better than he could have. "Tell Agatha I said hello. Sheriff, I will text you should something out of the ordinary arise."

Without waiting for either of the men to respond, Stan lifted his teacup and saucer from the table and carried them out to the kitchen. A silent, grim-faced Marilyn took the dishes from him.

"Are you all right, Marilyn?" Stan asked.

"Quite," she replied, her tone stiff, and Stan knew she was not.

"Ah," he said. He tried to think of something to follow that utterance, but when he failed to do so, he nodded goodnight and left the house.

It was a four-mile walk to the factory, and Stan needed to think about what he would do if there was a ghost at the building.

Adam walked into the kitchen and found Marilyn drying the dishes and putting them away. From the side door, he could see Stan stepping around the street corner and disappearing from view.

"May I ask a question?" Adam inquired.

Marilyn glanced over her shoulder and gave him a nod and a small smile.

"Has Stan always been like this? Kind of a loner? Little bit odd? I know it comes out hard, I just can't think of another way to phrase it."

"You said it just fine, Adam." Marilyn dried her hands on a dish towel and sat down at a small table set in the corner. She motioned for Adam to join her, and he did so.

"To answer your question simply," Marilyn began. "No. He was not always like this. He was a different young man, but that was because home was a challenge for him. When he turned eighteen, he joined the Army and that was the last we saw of him for quite some time. He returned to us in 1994, and he was not the man who had left. Have you seen his scars?"

"A few," Adam admitted.

"Well, he has more than a few. Quite a bit more." Marilyn looked down at her hands for a moment, gave a tight smile and then raised her eyes again. "He was wounded in Iraq. Not even while fighting. Someone had left a trap, and Stan had set it off. It injured him quite a bit, and by the time he came home, he was angry. Angrier than when he left and far more dangerous. No one's quite sure where he learned to fight. A few veterans, like Kenny, said some of it would have been in basic training, but what Stan had picked up, well, that was a bit more. At first, he was hell on wheels. He fought anything and everything that came across his path. Stan was feared up and down the state and from side to side as well. He could fight, and what was more, he liked it."

"He doesn't seem to anymore," Adam said.

Marilyn smiled a soft expression with a hint of sadness. "No. And that's a sad story. He was in Dow's one night, as was my son. Stan had a good drunk on, there's no other way to put it, and he was minding his business at the bar. My son was recently divorced, and his ex-wife's new boyfriend was feeling his oats. The ex-wife and the new boyfriend sat close to Damon, my boy, and picked a fight, the boyfriend drawing a pistol."

Marilyn cleared her throat, wiped at her eyes and then continued.

"Stan wouldn't allow it," she said. "He stepped between Damon and the others. Three things happened. Damon's ex-wife slapped Stan, so Stan knocked her out with a punch to the nose. And then her new boyfriend pulled the trigger of the gun he'd brought with him."

Marilyn paused, gathered her thoughts and spoke in a low voice. "The bullet passed through Stan's left arm and buried itself in Damon's heart."

She shook her head. "A few other patrons of the bar tackled the boyfriend and took the gun away from him. Stan tried to save my boy. But there was no saving him. Damon was gone."

"I'm sorry," Adam managed to say.

Marilyn nodded. "Thank you. It happened quite some time ago, Adam. The pain is always here, of course. Stan lives with me because he was willing to die for Damon. You'll find that as you go through town, there are quite a few people who are indebted to Stanley Owens for one reason or another. One day, you should ask Mack what Stan did for him. You'll understand why Stan eats for free. But Stan, well, he's been a fixture here for over twenty years now. He's seen quite a bit, and I think the only person who really knew about it was Kenny. Kenny's death won't sit well with Stan, and I suspect there'll be hell to pay."

Adam could only nod his agreement, his voice failing him.

CHAPTER 28

HYACINTH AND THE FACTORY

Stan stood outside the factory and looked across the back parking lot. He had thoroughly searched the side lot and found nothing. Not even the faintest hint of a ghost. He had watched and listened, felt the air around each vehicle and listened for the telltale beep of a security system failing because of the battery being drained.

He let his eyes wander, looking for shimmers and incomplete forms.

And he found it.

A shimmer off to the far left, just inside the tree line where there shouldn't have been a shimmer of any sort. The moon hid behind the clouds, and the lights of the parking lot did not illuminate that far in.

Stan walked along the perimeter of the parking lot, his eyes locked onto the shimmer.

It stayed in place, and as he drew nearer, he saw it begin to take form. The ghost of a woman looked out at the factory as though waiting for someone to exit. She was small, and Stan knew her hands would be proportionate to the rest of her body.

A small ghost with small hands. A hand, he had no doubt, whose print would match up perfectly with the one on Finn Reddington's neck.

She was not, however, the ghost he had seen in Kenny's house. That one had been larger and undeniably male.

More importantly, she paid no attention to Stan.

He was nearly upon her when she finally became aware of his presence. She glanced over one shoulder, then started to look back to the factory when she stopped, fully aware that he was focused on her.

The dead woman took a cautious step to one side, her eyes locked on him.

"You can see me, then," she stated.

"Yes," Stan confirmed, stopping half a dozen feet from her.

"What is it you want, then?"

"I want you to leave," Stan told her. "You should not be here. There should not be any of the dead here. This place was made free of the dead long before I ever arrived."

Her lip curled in a sneer, and she let out an unpleasant laugh. "I care not for what was, only for what is. And that, boy, is what you see standing before you. Strange, you can see me. Not many who can. I'll give you to the count of twenty to get on out, seeing as how I'm in a charitable mood."

Stan raised an eyebrow at the statement, but he did not move.

"That's how it is, then?" she asked, a note of pleasure in her voice.

"It is."

"Good."

Stan planted his feet, braced himself and watched as the dead woman sprinted at him. She struck a heartbeat later, his body rocking with the impact even as she vanished from in of him. His flesh stung where she had touched him, and his heart rate quickened.

She reappeared a few moments later and almost twenty feet from him to the left. He caught only the faintest glow from her, and he turned to face her again.

"Well, then," she grumbled. "That was not a pleasant experience. What's wrong with you, boy?"

"There is nothing wrong with me," Stan answered.

"I've touched many and many," she said, waggling a finger at him. "Nary a one of them did that to me. 'Tain't nothin' but iron has made me feel that."

Her eyes narrowed. "That's it, innit? Iron? You wearing it, then?"

She took a step forward, and Stan waited.

"No," she said, answering her own question. "Can't see it, and it'd have to be close to a shirt to do what it did. Where is it, then, boy?"

Stan gave a small shake of the head. "I am not willing to tell you."

"I can make you tell me," she replied, taking a step closer. "Won't be pleasant. I can guarantee you that."

"I do not think that will be the case in this particular instance."

The dead woman advanced toward him, and Stan let her. He dropped his hands to his sides and waited. His eyes never left her as she stepped closer, cold engulfing him and causing him to shiver. The dead woman's power vibrated around her, pulsating as it burrowed into his bones.

Stan held himself still as she reached out for his right hand. The flesh was tanned and, more importantly, absent of any jewelry. It was, as far as the dead woman was concerned, free of anything that might be made of iron.

"This will hurt," she grinned, licking her lips. "And I'll enjoy that."

Stan nodded.

The dead woman reached out, taking her time, watching his expression as she hesitated a moment before clasping his hand in her own.

Her shriek died almost as soon as it escaped her lips, and the woman vanished into the darkness. When she reappeared, it was close to where she had reappeared before.

She glared at him. "There's something not right with you, boy."

"More than likely, that's true," Stan agreed. He stepped toward her, and she eased back several more steps.

"Nay, you'll not touch me," she stated. "Not until I know a bit more about you, then, boy. Understood?"

"Come with me," he urged. "We can speak all you want. I will be happy to answer any questions you might have."

She shook her head. "Nay. I've a job to do, and none can say Hyacinth don't finish them. I don't know what it is you're about, boy, but I'll find out soon enough."

Stan took another step toward her, and the dead woman vanished.

Stan looked around the woods. The trees were young here, but the leaf cover was heavy. In addition to that, he knew the dead could have a wide range to roam, especially if they were strong.

He had a suspicion that she was strong. She'd been more frustrated than frightened by the natural repulsion formed by the iron in his skin.

He glanced around the trees once more, part of him wanting to search the ground for whatever item she might be connected to, but he knew it was worse than the proverbial needle in a haystack. At least with the haystack, he knew he'd be looking for a needle.

Not so with Hyacinth.

He had no idea as to what she might be bound to, and without that knowledge, the search would be futile.

One solid piece of information had come out about the situation. There was a ghost at the factory, and that ghost should not have been there. Not at the factory.

It was well past midnight when Stan stepped into the parlor and found Adam asleep in one of the chairs.

Stan sat down across from him, took a sip from the glass of water he had poured in the kitchen a moment before, and considered waking Adam. The younger man snored, shifted and then startled awake.

"Damn," Adam mumbled, straightening up and rubbing his eyes. "You been there long?"

"Not at all," Stan answered. "Only a minute or so. I had thought of waking you, but you came awake anyway."

"Well, I've been waiting," Adam said, stifling a yawn.

"You would like to know about where I went?"

"Where you went, what you saw, and what you did," Adam confirmed.

"I went to the factory," Stan stated. "I saw a ghost. I watched her leave."

Adam frowned. "Okay. You went to the factory to try and see the ghost, which you managed to do."

Stan nodded. "It was easy. She was not trying to hide. Like most of the dead, she did not initially believe anyone could see her. This was a mistaken belief."

"Seems like it," Adam nodded. "So, she didn't hide from you at all?"

"No," Stan confirmed. "I was too close to her when she acknowledged that I could see her. She did attempt to harm me and drive me off. It did not work. She tried again, and once more, she failed. I had hoped to capture her, but she is too smart."

"How so?" Adam asked.

"When she understood I could see her, when she understood that she could not stop me with a touch, then she came to realize I might be able to take her, should I find her item. And so, she left."

"Could she be the ghost of a worker?" Adam asked.

Stan shook his head. "There are no ghosts there. Not anymore, at least. Well, not until her arrival."

"You're sure about that?" Adam asked. "I don't mean to imply anything."

"I know you do not," Stan assured him. "I know there are no ghosts there because I am the one who removed them in 2002. The factory was defunct at the time, and it was partly due to a trio of ghosts who had died there. They did not appreciate anyone running the machines, and so they made it impossible to work the job. I was approached in September of 2002, and I was asked to remove the dead from the building. The town was in desperate straits. Work was needed, and I agreed. I moved the dead, and the people worked."

"How did she get there?" Adam shook his head. "It doesn't make any sense."

"Someone placed her there," Stan informed him. "She is there to enforce control, to ensure the workers follow their instructions. It is an interesting way to control the working population. But that leads us to who has brought the dead woman in to control the workers. Was it the manager of the factory? Was it the owner? Perhaps it was a third group interested in seeing the company work beyond projections. We do not know, Adam, and we need to know if we are going to stop it."

"We need to stop it," Adam murmured.

"We do," Stan nodded. "Whoever brought in the dead is responsible for Kenny's death."

Adam's eyes widened.

"They are. And I suspect for the passing of Annie Hamm and Omer L'Étrange, as well. They must be held accountable for these attacks and for the attack on Finn Reddington."

"How do we find who did it?" Adam asked. "How do we track down someone putting a ghost near a factory?"

"It's not just one ghost, Adam," Stan sighed. "It is at least two, and possibly more."

Adam shook his head. "What?"

"The attack at the factory was done by a woman," Stan explained. "The attack on Kenny was done by a man. There are at least two."

"Two," Adam said, shaking his head. "As if one wouldn't be bad enough."

Ezra pulled into the back parking lot of his factory, shut his car down and made sure his phone was secured in its Faraday pouch. With that done, he exited the vehicle and headed towards the direction where he had left Hyacinth's ring.

He was in a few feet of it when she appeared, a foul look on her face and anger in her voice.

"Did you know about a witness?" she demanded.

Ezra stopped, confused. "What? A witness? Are you talking about a religious witness or something?"

"No, I'm not talking about something as trifling as that," she snapped. "I'm talking about one who can see the dead freely, and not a child then either. Do you understand? Tis a man who sees the dead when they do not wish to be seen, then."

Ezra shook his head. "Are you telling me there are people who can see ghosts all the time?"

She let out an exasperated groan. "I know I'm speakin' the King's English, so why aren't you hearin' it? Yes, a witness sees the dead. They've the sight that most lose with their childhood. There's a man here, and he can see me plain as day. And he cannot be touched."

"What?" Ezra's voice was tight as fear gripped him. "What do you mean by that, Hyacinth?"

"I went to strike him," she stated. "When I did, I was knocked back into my ring. It took a moment for me to gather my wits about me and another moment to decide what to do. I decided it was nothing more than a freak incident. Perhaps he wore a bit of iron, perhaps even a piece of iron armor 'neath his shirt."

"Was he wearing it?" Ezra asked.

"No," she answered. "There were no telltale signs of it. Not even a hint. I saw that clear enough as I went to touch him again. The man did not move, Ezra. Not a hair on him shifted as I moved in close. He had no fear, and he let me grasp his hand. Next I knew, the pain I felt tore a shriek from my dead throat and put me back in the damned ring once more. He is a witness, and he is untouchable. I suspect he searches for you, Ezra Pettigrew. That he searches for the one who put me here."

"And why do you think that?" Ezra asked, keeping fear out of his own voice.

"He said he had questions," Hyacinth answered. "And the only questions that would make sense would be those about the dead."

"Stay clear of him," Ezra said.

The dead woman laughed. "I'll do my best, then, but have no doubt he'll find me if he wants me. I cannot hide and be about your work. Put your ear to the ground, Ezra, and find out who around here can speak with the dead. 'Tis as simple as that. Until then, I'll be here, waiting on word from you as to who needs speaking to next."

The dead woman faded from view, and Ezra was left standing alone.

He remained there for several minutes, then turned and returned to his car. He had his own questions to ask and answers that needed to be found.

CHAPTER 29

THE BURIAL

They buried Kenny on Saturday morning.

Kenny's service took place in Edgewood Cemetery in Nashua, New Hampshire. Stan stood off to one side as the pastor from the First Congregationalist Church said the prayers and spoke words of comfort for those gathered. Most of the people at the funeral had worked with Kenny or knew him from Alcoholics Anonymous and other organizations. Stan knew some of them from town, but most were strangers to him. He was not gregarious like Kenny had been.

Stan did not appreciate the company of others.

As the coffin was lowered into the grave, Stan turned away from it. He had, for the first time in years, driven his own vehicle. The battered pickup was parked at the top of the cemetery, far from the hearse and the line of cars behind it.

The narrow roads in Edgewood were rippled and cracked from long years of frost heaves and heavy equipment moving earth and stones. A well-built chapel stood off to the left, and on the slight hill rising up to meet the granite steps of the building sat a man and a young girl. It took Stan only a moment to understand that the girl was a ghost and the man was alive.

And they were talking to one another.

As he neared them, the girl faded away, and the man took out a pack of cigarettes. A moment later, the cigarette was lit, and smoke curled out of the stranger's nostrils, moving up and around his bald head. Stan saw the scars on the man's harsh features, the missing bit of ear on one side, and then the realization that the man was completely and utterly hairless.

"Morning," the stranger greeted.

Stan stopped, held his hands behind his back and replied, "Good morning. Where did your friend go?"

"What friend is that?" the stranger asked, tapping the head off his cigarette into the grass and tapping down the ashes with his foot.

"The young girl who was here," Stan answered. "It is not often I see someone speaking to a ghost."

"You saw that, huh?" the man asked, flashing a smile of missing teeth. Those that remained were slightly crooked and stained. "Well, you're right. She's a friend of mine. She died back in the nineties. My name's Shane, by the way. Shane Ryan."

Stan shook Shane's hand. "A pleasure to meet you. My name is Stan Owens."

"Friend of yours?" Shane asked, nodding in the direction of Kenny's grave.

Stan considered the question for a moment, then replied, "I think he was my best friend."

"I'm sorry."

"So am I," Stan sighed.

"Want to take a seat?"

Stan wanted to say no, but he found himself sitting down beside the man.

"Does the cigarette bother you?" Shane asked.

"No," Stan answered. "I smoked for several years when I was younger."

"Was it hard to quit?"

Stan shook his head.

Shane took a long drag off his cigarette and turned his head away to exhale the smoke. "How'd you do it?"

"I ended up in a hospital," Stan stated. "It was frowned upon."

Shane chuckled. "Yeah. I find I can usually sneak in a couple of smokes if I'm in a hospital, though."

"I did not think I would be able to do so. It was a military hospital."

"Oh yeah?" Shane faced him once more. "Which one?"

"Walter Reed," Stan told him, shifting his attention back to Kenny's grave. People were walking away, and in a far corner of the cemetery, Stan saw a pickup with gravediggers waiting to complete their task.

"Were you there as family or as a service member?"

"Service member," Stan answered.

"Wounded or injured?"

Stan looked at Shane. "I was wounded. Improvised explosive devices, as they call them now. It was on the highway of death in Iraq."

"That was a little before my time," Shane chuckled. "I think I was just wrapping up high school. Maybe bootcamp, I'm not sure."

"You were a Marine, then?"

Shane nodded. "You?"

"Army." Stan took a deep breath and then let it out at a slow, measured pace. "I still carry a lot of shrapnel in me."

"Must make traveling fun," Shane observed.

Stan smiled softly. "If I flew anywhere, you would be correct. However, I do not travel."

"How did your friend die, if you don't mind my asking?"

"I do not mind," Stan answered. "Officially, the papers state it was a failed suicide attempt, one that inevitably killed him."

"Officially?"

"Yes," Stan said.

"And I take it that means you disagree with the cause of death?"

"Yes," Stan muttered. "Kenny would not kill himself. I have no doubt, though, that he was murdered by a ghost."

Shane stubbed out his cigarette, fieldstripped his cigarette butt and stuffed the papers into his pocket.

"I am sorry," Stan sighed. "I did not mean to bother you, I assumed you were aware that ghosts could harm you since I saw you sitting with your dead friend."

"Oh, no, you assumed correctly," Shane responded. "I believe you completely. I've dealt with a few difficult ghosts before. I kind of have a hobby of dealing with them. So, if you need any sort of help, you can give me a call or come on over. Either one works fine. Do you have a cellphone?"

"No," Stan answered. "But I can write it down."

He took a small notebook out of his pocket, and Shane chuckled. "Okay. Here's my number, and then I'll give you my address."

Stan listened and wrote down both as Shane gave them to him, and when Shane finished, Stan read them back to him.

"Squared away," Shane chuckled as Stan returned his pencil and notebook to his pocket.

"You will not be bothered if I should call you, then?" Stan asked, feeling uncertain.

"Not at all," Shane responded with growing seriousness. "I know how hard it can be, looking for people to help you with a problem. Especially when that problem is the dead, there are only so many people you can turn to. I'd like to be one of them."

"An admirable goal," Stan remarked.

Shane snorted. "Glad you think so."

Stan glanced over his shoulder and saw the last of the cars pulling out of the cemetery's front gate.

"This is a gentle place," Stan remarked.

"It usually is," Shane agreed. "It's a good place to think, and the dead enjoy their peace and quiet. They try to keep it that way, too."

Stan looked around, then asked, "Do you think they will mind if I come here, on occasion? I suspect if I were to find a quiet place in Mason, others would quickly interrupt me. Although, it will require me to drive."

"They probably won't mind," Shane said. "And you don't like to drive?"

"I do not," Stan answered, shifting his attention back to Shane. "It reminds me of the highway of death."

"Being wounded?"

"No," Stan replied. "All of the dead and the way the burnt flesh stank."

CHAPTER 30
AT THE DINER

Sweat clung to James' pale face, and Ezra wondered if he might have to bring someone else in to handle the delicate task of getting the factory back under control.

As soon as the thought finished, though, Ezra discarded it. James was already in too deep, as the saying went, and Ezra would much rather sacrifice one element of his management team than two. There were other men and women who could perform admirably and, without a doubt, better under pressure, but Ezra would work with what he had.

He needed to.

"Do you think it's safe for us to speak like this?" James asked.

Ezra put down his fork and looked at the man.

"James," Ezra began, choosing his words carefully. "You and I are eating in a restaurant, and we are discussing managerial concerns. Nothing more. If anyone remembers us, they will remember a pair of ordinary middle class men of middle age talking about the humdrum of running a business when the workers are being difficult. Stop jumping at shadows."

James cleared his throat. "Yes, sir."

"Good, now, talk to me about the trio of individuals causing an issue on the first shift."

"Yes, sir." James took a drink of water. "The Corville cousins. They've been making a lot of noise about wanting better pay for an increase in production. Today, they're in town for a bowling tournament. They skipped mandatory overtime for it."

Ezra frowned. "Did they ask permission?"

"No," James answered, and color returned to his cheeks. A deep, angry crimson. "They didn't. And when I told them they needed to, they laughed at me and, well, they threatened to beat me up."

"That's unacceptable behavior," Ezra muttered. He stabbed a piece of steak with his fork, brought the meat to his mouth and chewed for a moment before adding, "They'll have to be spoken to."

James nodded.

"Bowling tournament in Mason?" Ezra asked after he swallowed the mouthful.

"Yes. I overheard them saying they were going to eat at the diner and then make their way to the Mason's gun club. They have new rifles they want to sight in or some such nonsense."

Ezra hid his smile behind another bite of meat. James was clearly out of his depth dealing with the men and women of this particular factory, and Ezra would do well to remember it in the future. However, it was humorous to see the other man's reactions to the quintessential blue-collar life.

"That's good. We'll know where they are should we need it for documentation concerning their jobs," Ezra stated.

He had no intention of creating documentation, but the less James knew about the action Ezra was about to take, the better.

Ezra didn't think the man would hold up well under a police interrogation.

✷ ✷ ✷

Stan parked his truck in the small garage Leonard Washington had given to him years earlier. When he got out of the vehicle, he hung the ignition key on the pegboard beside the door and then inspected the garage. He checked that the windows were locked and that the pull-down door was secure. Other than the truck, he kept nothing in the garage. There was no reason to, and he had little enough.

Satisfied that the garage was in good shape, Stan left it and locked the small side door with the spare key he kept in his wallet. His stomach rumbled, a not-so-subtle reminder that it was well past his usual time for lunch, and he decided to go to the diner instead of back to Marilyn's. Changing out of his funeral clothes could wait. His body was telling him that lunch could not.

Stan set a quick pace for himself and moved along the sidewalks and the streets until he came up to Main Street and turned left. Ahead of him, he saw Mack's diner and increased his speed. When he reached the building, Alice opened the door for him.

"I saw you coming along at a hell of a pace for you, Stan Owens," she grinned, letting the door close as he passed her. "Go on to your usual seat. Don't pay any mind to the Corville boys. They just took second place at the tournament at Mickey's Glow and Bowl."

"Mr. Owens," one of the cousins called out. "We're second champions!"

The young men laughed, and Alice shook her head, smiling as they held miniature bowling trophies aloft.

Stan offered up a small smile. "That is quite the accomplishment, gentlemen. I congratulate you."

The men cheered and turned their attention back to their meals. Stan sat down in his regular place, and Alice gave him a pat on the shoulder. Leaning in, she said in a low voice, "You're getting better, you know."

"How is that?" Stan asked.

"When you interact with other people," she answered. "You're getting better at it."

Stan felt a strange sense of pride and settled back into the comfort of the seat as Alice went to bring him his tea.

✳ ✳ ✳

"I want them frightened," Ezra stated. "Not damaged. Is this understood?"

The ghost of Darryl Rarest looked askew at Ezra and seemed about to say something but clamped his mouth closed instead.

Ezra stared at the dead man. "Listen to me, Darryl. I have no qualms about sending you back. I have been assured that you will be dealt with accordingly, should I have to do so. The choice is yours, obviously. Do as I ask, and enjoy your freedom with me, or do not, and return from whence you came."

The dead man rolled his eyes, folded his arms over his chest and asked, "How frightened?"

"Enough so that they return to work and stop this nonsense," Ezra answered.

"How much damage can I do, if necessary?"

"You may break things around them," Ezra replied through clenched teeth. "You may not break any part of the workers. Is this clear?"

"Very much so," the dead man grumbled. "Where are they?"

"Walk up until you see a diner. Inside will be three young men. Apparently, according to my sources, they won some bowling competition. They were awarded plastic trophies."

"Sure, sure," Darryl nodded. "You'll be here?"

"No," Ezra answered. "I'll be driving up on the other side of the street in a moment. I want to sit and watch the show. I'd like to see how you work."

The dead man laughed. "You'll get a kick out of it. I'll let them know this wouldn't have happened if they were at work."

Before Ezra could respond, the dead man vanished.

With a sigh, Ezra hurried toward the diner. He had no wish to miss the show.

*** *** ***

Stan finished his tea, straightened up and then looked to the door as a chill entered the diner.

A dead man, short and with the appearance of a rodent, slipped through the door. He paused, glanced around the diner, and then made his way toward the booth with the Corville Cousins.

The dead man strolled up the aisle, and as he did so, Stan swung out his left hand.

The ghost paid him no attention, but his eyes widened, and he snarled as Stan's hand passed through and he vanished.

Stan waited a moment, and when the dead man did not immediately return, Stan stood up.

"Mack," he called, and Mack appeared a moment later in the doorway to the kitchen.

"What's up?"

"Take everyone out," Stan ordered.

Mack hesitated, then nodded. "Alice, gather up the Corville boys while I turn off the burners. Out the front or back, Stan?"

"I would advise using the back door," Stan answered.

As Alice hurried the Corvilles and an older couple Stan didn't recognize into the kitchen, Stan walked to the counter, went behind it and found a large container of salt. It was the same one he had seen Alice use in the past to refill the saltshakers on the tables in the booths and on the countertop.

Stan opened it and poured a long line across the pass-through between the kitchen and the counter area and then across the doorway leading into the kitchen. Satisfied with the rudimentary protection the salt would provide, at least for a short time, Stan stepped over to the main entrance and waited.

Several minutes passed, and just as he believed the dead man was not returning, the ghost came in. The small dead man wore an expression of confused anger as he hurried past Stan.

Stan poured a thick line of salt across the diner's entrance, set the container down and turned to face the ghost.

The dead man went from booth to booth, the confusion vanishing from his expression.

"Everyone is gone," Stan informed the ghost.

The dead man ignored him.

Stan cleared his throat. "I am speaking to you, sir. The ghost looking into the booths."

The dead man stiffened, straightened up, and, for the first time, took notice of Stan.

Without moving, the ghost asked, "Can you really see me?"

"Easily," Stan answered.

"Huh." The dead man scratched his chin as the anger faded from his face, then asked, "What's your name?"

"Stan, and yours?"

The ghost peered at him for a moment, shrugged and replied, "Darryl."

"It is a pleasure to meet you, Darryl."

The dead man snorted his disbelief at the statement. "Where'd those boys get off to?"

"The Corville cousins are gone," Stan answered.

"I can see that," Darryl sneered. "Wasn't what I asked. Where'd they get off to?"

"I do not know," Stan informed him. "I did not ask."

"Suppose you told them to get on out, though?"

Stan nodded.

"I know they didn't go out the front," Darryl mused. "Guess that means they went out the back. Well, been interesting, Stan. Hope not to see you around."

Stan didn't respond. Instead, he watched the ghost walk toward the kitchen door.

When the dead man reached it, Darryl let out a hiss and took a quick step back. Stan watched as the ghost looked at the floor and then shook his head in disbelief. Darryl's head lifted, turned toward the pass-through and saw the line of salt there, too. The ghost shifted his position, looked at the entrance and let out a cold, bitter laugh.

"Well, that's a hell of a sight," Darryl admitted. "Been a long time since I saw salt lines. In fact, last time I did, I was caught by them."

The dead man turned and glared at Stan. There was no humor or interest in his expression. In fact, there was no emotion whatsoever.

"Is that what you plan on doing, Stan?" Darryl inquired. "You thinkin' you're going to take me in?"

"No," Stan answered. "I have no interest in taking you right now."

"But you think it's somethin' you can do, huh?" Darryl's hands clenched and relaxed compulsively.

"I know it is. That is not the purpose of the salt, however," Stan stated. "I have several questions I would like answers to."

"And if I don't answer them?" the dead man asked.

"Then we might run into some issues," Stan remarked.

"That's an understatement."

Before Stan could respond, the dead man stepped up to the counter, took hold of a napkin dispenser and sent it hurtling toward Stan.

Shifting his weight to his left foot and turning, Stan watched as the heavy dispenser sailed past him, crashing into the wall behind him.

Glasses, salt and pepper shakers, mugs and plates, flatware and bottles soared through the air at Stan. While he did his best to avoid many of them, more than a few struck him.

Confronting this particular ghost, it seemed, had been a poorly conceived plan.

Stan was ill-prepared. He would not, he understood, achieve his goal of getting questions answered.

The ghost sent several water glasses racing toward him, and Stan avoided all but one. That one, however, struck him in the side of the head as he turned away and sent him to his knees.

From the corner of his eye, Stan saw the dead man sprint toward him, and all Stan could do was hold up his hand, arm extended, as though he was trying to stop traffic.

The dead man ran into Stan's hand and vanished.

✳ ✳ ✳

It wasn't the show he expected.

In fact, it wasn't a show at all.

After Darryl had entered the restaurant, Ezra had watched the people come racing around the back of the diner, and then hurry across the street and into what looked like the public library.

After a few minutes, he saw Darryl stalk across the street and back into the diner.

Confused, Ezra watched the scene unfold through the diner's large, plate glass windows. He had seen Darryl exchanging words with a living man in the restaurant, and then the dead man had begun throwing things.

Lots of them, too.

The living man hadn't been able to stop all of the objects, and when he finally went down, Ezra watched as Darryl charged at his opponent.

And when he reached the living man, Darryl had vanished.

Something was wrong, Ezra realized as he started his rental.

Something was terribly wrong.

CHAPTER 31
PHILOMENA

He stood within the safety of the salt lines, and he waited.

It was four hours since the attack in the diner, and Stan was in a significant amount of pain. He knew it could have been worse, but it did not diminish the pain he felt.

He also would not be able to treat any of his injuries until he spoke with Philomena.

Stan knew he didn't know any of her routines. She might not creep out of the house until long after night had fallen, and he might not gain her insight regarding the assailants he had seen while that information might still be useful.

"I've seen you far too much lately, Stanley Owens," Philomena complained.

"The feeling is mutual, Philomena," Stan assured her. "I have come, though, regarding help in finding those who killed Kenny."

The dead woman fixed her attention on him as she drifted closer to the barrier that separated them. "Have you found them?"

"So far, I have identified a large male ghost, a small male ghost, and a small female one."

"Tell me what they have all done," Philomena ordered. "Tell me why you think they have done it."

Stan did as he was bade, and soon he was finished. He sat in silence.

"You will need to be violent," she told him after a few minutes.

"I do not wish to be violent."

Philomena laughed. "If you want resolution for the crimes committed, and to prevent any others from occurring, you will have to resort to violence. Nothing else will solve this."

"Violence against the dead often has a tendency to affect the living as well," Stan informed her.

"I am already dead," Philomena reminded him. "Dead, and the only person I cared for has been murdered. I do not care, Stanley Owens, what sort of moral quandary you find yourself in regarding the injuring of humans. In order to move forward, you must speak with the man running the factory. You must ask him questions, and, in the parlance of your grandfather, you must ask them hard."

Stan closed his eyes for a moment. "I have done this before."

"Have you?"

He heard the doubt in her voice and opened his eyes to look at the dead woman.

"I have been a violent man, Philomena," he said. "I have done violence for the sake of violence. Killed, at times, because the man needed killing. That was a long, long time ago. My hands have healed, although my heart has not. I do not wish to return to that place."

"Let me ask you this question," Philomena said in a low voice. "Do you want those who murdered Kenny to go free, or do you want them punished for their crime?"

Stan stood up, brushed the dirt off himself and looked at his dead relative.

Then, he nodded and said a single word as he turned away.

"Punished."

CHAPTER 32
UNWANTED ATTENTION

Ezra sat in the office of his suite, wrapped in a thick robe with a glass of white wine in one hand. Three of the ghosts stood across from him, Theo, Darryl, and Hyacinth. Ezra had an unsettling feeling in the pit of his stomach, and the wine was doing little to help it. All three of the dead had described roughly the same man who had interacted with them.

Darryl had extricated himself from the situation, which was fine, but the living man had asked the ghosts questions. The living man had, in fact, gone so far as to trap Darryl in the diner until the dead man came into contact with him.

"And he wasn't wearing any jewelry, correct?" Ezra asked Darryl again.

"Are you deaf?" Darryl snarled. "I said he wasn't wearing iron. I would have seen it. You can't miss it. Besides, I only touched his damned hand. It's not like I ran through him and hit some sort of necklace."

Ignoring Darryl's attitude, Ezra shifted his attention to Hyacinth. "Were you able to see if he was wearing anything on his fingers or his wrists?"

She shook her head.

Ezra glanced at Theo, and the dead man stated, "I kept about as far from him as I could."

"This person is problematic," Ezra sighed. "Well, thank you all for speaking with me. If you would like to retire to your objects, please do so."

The ghosts took it for the dismissal it was meant to be, and Ezra sipped at his wine as he shifted his position in the chair to fix his gaze on the blank wall in front of him. He let his eyes slip out of focus and his mind wander. It was often the best remedy for problems.

Solitude and no distractions.

Unconsciously, he drank more of his wine, his thoughts meandering along the basic problem of the stranger.

"Who is he?" Ezra wondered aloud.

Who was the man? Where did he live? What was his connection to Mason? Why was he interfering with Ezra's plans? Could it be intentional?

Ezra shook his head at the last question as it rumbled past.

How could the man be intentionally interfering with Ezra's plans? Only James knew of Ezra's method of correction for Mason, New Hampshire. And James, Ezra knew, was too loyal to betray him.

Still, the man needed to be identified.

Ezra would not be able to use the ghosts he had already deployed. They were known to this stranger. Known and searched for.

Perhaps, Ezra mused, he could use Lars. The dead man was a giant, but he would be a new factor. All Ezra needed was for the ghost to track down the stranger. Once that was done, a solution to that particular problem could be found.

He would need to speak with Lars.

But not until he finished his wine.

Taking another sip, Ezra closed his eyes and did his best to relax.

Stan sat in his workshop behind Marilyn's house, and Adam sat with him.

"What is it?" Adam asked.

Stan looked at the young man and considered his response. Finally, he said, "I am afraid I must become violent."

Adam blinked. "What?"

Stan nodded. "I went in search of advice. Unfortunately, I found that advice to be sound. I am going to need to commit an act of violence against another person."

Adam was silent for a short time. Then, in a slightly confused tone, he asked, "Do you mean violent like the other night when those guys tried to jump me at Dow's?"

"Similar, but not the same," Stan answered.

"How?"

Stan looked at his hands, turning them over to look at the scars along their backs.

"The fight in the bar," Stan began, "was not planned. Oh, what happened when the fight began was planned. There are reactions to situations that are ingrained, not in your muscles, but rather in your memory. You train so much that your intellectual reactions occur at a subconscious level. So, yes, in that way, the fight at Dow's was planned, but you can say it was planned decades ago when I learned how to fight properly."

Stan paused, and Adam waited.

"This violence I am going to commit will be different," Stan explained. "It will be designed to deliver pain, to instill fear of the pain to come, and the horror of what failure to cooperate will bring forth."

"Oh."

Silence fell over them again, and Stan found himself focusing on the smell of wood in his workshop.

After a few moments of silence, he said, "I need to visit the new manager at the factory where Kenny worked."

"Do you want me to come along?" Adam asked, and Stan was pleased there was no fear in the young man's voice.

"No. I do not want you close to that violence."

"Why do you have to talk to him?" Adam asked. "Is it just because

Kenny worked there?"

"Kenny worked there, Annie worked there, and Omer did as well. Finn Reddington, who was attacked at the factory, obviously works there. And the three Corville cousins who were the targets of yesterday's attempted attack at the diner, they work there as well."

"Not to be a doubting Thomas here, Stan," Adam said. "But doesn't most of the town work at the factory?"

Stan gave him a small smile. "You are quite correct. However, those I mentioned were all, well, troublemakers. Kenny, I learned, was leading the resistance against new policies put in place by the factory's new owner. Annie and Omer led their shifts in the same way. Finn was due to step into a position of leadership, and he is not, or was not, the type of man to bend easily to management. And, finally, the Corville cousins are, to put it mildly, difficult at the best of times. They had been extremely vocal about their dislike of management's new practices. So, all these people have two things in common. First, they all were, or are, employed by the factory. Second, they were trouble. Who is affected by a quarrelsome workforce?"

"Management," Adam answered.

Stan nodded. "Management indeed. And since that is the case, who should I speak to about the situation?"

"Management."

"Yes," Stan murmured. He rubbed his hands together for a moment and then looked at Adam. "I am going to find who management is and where they are. When I do, I am going to ask that person some questions, Adam. I am going to ask them hard. It will not be pleasant to witness, and I will not have you labeled as an accomplice because you were there. I will ask the hard questions, Adam. I will do the hard work."

"What should I do?"

"Call Agatha," Stan smiled. "I suspect the two of you might enjoy some time together. Marilyn holds my money for me, I will ask her to give you a bit for a good night on the town."

"Stan," Adam grinned, "I can afford to pay my own way. I'm working."

"Consider it an advance on your assistance with my boxes," Stan responded. "Or merely for serving as a sounding board. The fact remains; I would like you to have a good time."

"And what about you?" Adam asked. "When are you going to try and locate the manager at the factory?"

"Now," Stan replied and got to his feet.

✳ ✳ ✳

Mr. Pettigrew had purchased a small house in Amherst, New Hampshire, for James' use. It was a perk of James' employment with the company and a sign of how much confidence Mr. Pettigrew had in him.

James had asked why he hadn't been provided with a home closer to the factory for the simple sake of convenience should an issue arise. Mr. Pettigrew smiled and informed him, "Delegating authority and minimizing the need for micromanagement is the only way to make a business profitable. You must have foremen and shift leaders you can rely on. If you can't, then fire them and find someone else."

James reflected on this as he poured himself a glass of a pre-mixed margarita and carried it into the living room. The house had come furnished with non-descript items easily found in big-box stores and lacked any sort of personality.

That was fine with James.

He didn't want a house with a personality. He wanted a house where he could relax far from the stresses of the day.

And if he was being honest with himself, James thought as he sipped his drink, work was becoming far more stressful than he ever believed it would.

He shuddered at the thought of Kenny's death and the fact that someone had snuck into the factory and beaten Finn Reddington in the men's room. What was worse, though, was the knowledge that Mr. Pettigrew had something to do with the incidents.

All James could hope for was a quick resolution to the problem. The sooner everything was done and the profits made, the sooner he could move on to another assignment. If he did well enough, James knew Mr. Pettigrew would reward him.

Smiling at the thought of where such a reward might land him, James took another drink of his margarita, only to lower it a moment later when the doorbell rang.

Frowning, he glanced at the time.

A quarter to nine.

James shook his head. He didn't know anyone in town, and he certainly wasn't going to allow some stranger to come into his home. No, there was no need to answer the door. Whoever it was would go away soon enough, and if not, James could always call the police.

The stranger at the door didn't go away.

The doorbell rang again and again.

By the tenth ring, James had finished his margarita, and he didn't feel like calling the police.

Instead, he stood up on wobbly legs and made his way to the front door. He was going to deal with the problem himself.

James unlocked the door and pulled it open.

CHAPTER 33
QUESTIONS AND ANSWERS

Stan closed and locked the door behind him. He turned out the porch light, then took hold of James Beckinsale's arms and dragged the man into the home's interior until he found the bathroom.

Sweat dripped down Stan's back by the time he finished getting James into the bathtub and securing him as best he could. From a plastic shopping bag, he removed a roll of duct tape, a large plastic drop sheet for painting, and then a pair of heavy, 3D-printed knuckledusters made from plastic filament. The knuckles were black, and small, pointed ridges rose up on the exposed portions.

While they would not be as damaging to James as a pair of actual brass knuckles, Stan hoped they would still serve their purpose.

He glanced around the bathroom and knew that the plastic and his other precautions were only perfunctory at best. Trace evidence would be gathered if the assault was reported, but Stan suspected it would be kept under wraps.

James groaned, and his eyes fluttered open. He looked around, slowly becoming aware of his situation. As he shifted his position in the tub and his eyes locked onto Stan, Stan knew James was not the one behind the death of Kenny and the others.

Not by any stretch of the imagination.

The man in the tub was nothing more than a tool for someone else.

"Good evening," Stan greeted.

"Who are you?" James whispered.

Stan shook his head. "I am going to explain some rather unfortunate rules to you, Mr. Beckinsale. First and most importantly, you are here to answer questions, not ask them. Second, if you do not answer a question, or should you forget the first rule, I will remind you. Painfully. Do you understand?"

"No." James tried to push himself farther away from Stan.

"A good, honest answer, Mr. Beckinsale," Stan informed him. "Continue to answer honestly, and this will be over very soon."

"What if I don't?" James asked, straightening up slightly.

Stan's right hand lashed out, the heavy knuckles smashing into the man's right shoulder and driving it into the shower tile, breaking one of them.

James let out a wail followed by a long, low whimper.

"You forgot the first rule, Mr. Beckinsale," Stan stated.

Standing up, Stan unfolded the plastic dropcloth and spread it out, taping it down as he went. He saw James' mouth open and close several times, as if he was about to ask a question each time and then decided against it.

It was, Stan knew, the best decision the other man could make. Stan did not want to hurt him, but he would do what was necessary.

Stan remembered his training, stepped close and struck James again, this time in a rib. The other man's breath rushed out and left him gasping for air.

"Now, Mr. Beckinsale, I will ask you again. Do you remember the first rule?"

James nodded, his face red. After a moment, he managed to whisper, "I think you broke a rib."

"I doubt that. More than likely," Stan replied. "I cracked it. Had I broken it, the rib would have pierced your lung, and this situation would be different. However, I am afraid I know my business. Now that we have once more established the essential rule to follow, I will ask you another question. Who do you work for, Mr. Beckinsale?"

James cleared his throat, his eyes darting around as though he expected the walls to be listening.

It was, Stan acknowledged, an interesting reaction from a man in the midst of torture.

"Time is a finite quantity, Mr. Beckinsale," Stan stated in a gentle voice. "This brings me to rule number three, which I did not want to mention, but here we are. Rule number three is do not make me repeat a question. Do you understand?"

James nodded. "I don't think I should tell you who my boss is."

"That is unfortunate," Stan replied, and he drove the knuckles into the man's ribs on the opposite side.

James squealed and wet himself as he collapsed against the side of the tub.

Stan sighed. "This is why we do this in a tub, Mr. Beckinsale. Inevitably, you will soil yourself. It is a natural reaction, I assure you, and it is nothing to be ashamed of. I have cracked another rib. My goal here is simple. To gather answers to several questions. If need be, I will hurt you to gain the information. I do not want to hurt you. Please understand this. As of right now, you have two cracked ribs, a mild concussion and, without a doubt, the beginnings of post-traumatic disorder. My goal is to leave here with the information, to leave you alive, and to carry out my task. Now, I am going to ask you who your employer is, and if you do not provide the name, I am going to hurt you again. I will continue to hurt you until I have the information I desire. If you understand me, please nod."

James nodded.

"Excellent, Mr. Beckinsale." Stan took a deep breath. "I want you to understand one other important piece of information about me. I was taught how to inflict pain. How to kill and to make it appear a suicide, or to make a body vanish completely. I do not want to employ any more of my skills this evening. So, I ask you, will you please tell me your employer's name?"

James Beckinsale shook his head.

Stan frowned and then applied rule number three.

Stan walked home with his hands behind his back and his attention elsewhere. It was, he knew, close to three in the morning. James Beckinsale had held out for an admirable length of time. Stan, for his part, was pleased he hadn't needed to break more than a few fingers. He had no love for the old job.

Not that he had enjoyed it when he was younger.

Stan had left James Beckinsale alive and as well as possible. True, there were the broken fingers, the cracked ribs and the multiple contusions, but the man was alive. He had set the man's fingers, wrapped his ribs, and placed him on the couch, sedated. The remainder of Stan's time there had been spent scouring the house. He knew he did not get all the evidence, which took far more preparation than he had given himself, but he felt comfortable knowing he had left the man alive. That, in and of itself, would ensure there would be no in-depth investigation.

If there was an investigation at all.

James Beckinsale planned to inform Ezra Pettigrew that he had fallen down an incline while hiking. It would account for most if not all the injuries, and Stan believed James Beckinsale could sell the act.

If he didn't, Stan would return.

He would return and make James Beckinsale's death appear to be a suicide, and Stan was far too skilled to make any amateur mistakes.

Still, Stan felt badly about injuring the man but shook the thought away as he reached his family's home. By the time he came to a stop on the driveway, Philomena was there.

"I remembered something," she said by way of greeting.

"And what was that?"

"When you were thirteen, your granduncle laughed after picking you up from school during the middle of the day," Philomena stated.

"Why do you think that was?" Stan already knew the answer.

"He said you were a quicker learner," she remarked. "I never thought much of it. Not until you mentioned your history of violence. I thought it the statement of a braggart."

"It was not, and I am not," Stan informed her.

"No," Philomena agreed. "It took me a short time to remember your granduncle had taken you into Manchester on more than one occasion, and Boston, too."

Stan nodded.

"You did work for him?"

"No," Stan answered. "I trained on men he needed to collect money from."

"I always wondered why you became tougher," Philomena mused. "After your first trip to Boston, I could never get quite the same reaction out of you when I beat you."

Stan felt the old anger rise up, and he pushed it down.

"This is not the conversation we should be having," he stated. "I have obtained the name of the man responsible for Kenny's death."

Philomena came as close to the line as she could.

"Who?" she hissed. "Who killed my godson?"

"A man named Ezra Pettigrew," Stan told her. "I will speak to him as soon as I can find him."

"You don't know where he is?!" she snapped.

"Patience, Philomena," he warned her. "Though we are at a truce here, it does not mean I am in any sort of mood for your temper."

She sneered at him.

"Find where this Pettigrew scum is hiding," Philomena grumbled. "And bring him to me. I would have words with him."

Stan considered responding to her. Instead, he turned and walked back down the driveway toward the road.

He was done with his relations for the night.

Now, he needed sleep, and it was still a long walk back to Marilyn's.

CHAPTER 34
BETTER CONTROL

Lars, Ezra saw, was far more skilled than anyone knew.

The dead man must have been ferocious when alive. The ghost's intellect was impressive and mirrored by a drive to succeed.

Ezra sat on a bench in a small park near a pond, on the surface of which Canadian geese floated. Lars sat beside him, silent. A young couple walked past them and smiled, and Ezra smiled in return.

To not exchange such a simple pleasantry would be remembered.

To return it would not.

Once the couple was well past them, Lars and Ezra continued their conversation.

"I'm supposed to only gather intelligence on this stranger, then?" Lars asked, repeating the basic instructions.

"Yes," Ezra confirmed. "However, I need as much information as possible."

The ghost chuckled. "Mr. Pettigrew, I can give you details on every person who has walked by us since you took me out of the bag. That is child's play. When I get a good enough look at this man, I'll be able to tell you every aspect about him. Hell, if I can, I'll find out where he lives and what type of toothpaste he uses."

Ezra smiled. "That, Lars, is precisely the type of detail I am looking for. Nothing, and I cannot stress this enough, nothing is too minute. Now, you must remember, according to your colleagues, this man also is able to see the dead. There is something about him, too, that causes your kind to be sent back to their objects when they touch him."

"I will do my best to remain unseen," Lars assured him. "If this turns out to be impossible, then I will act as though I do not see him. He should be used to that if he can truly see us."

"You doubt the others?"

"I doubt their ability to recognize when they make themselves known," Lars replied. "Some become more visible when they are, shall we say, worked up? That might be the case with the others. I don't know for certain, of course, but I'd rather play it that way. If I go in believing he can see us, that would be out of the ordinary for a ghost, would it not?"

Ezra smiled. "You are absolutely correct."

"So, unless he confronts me," Lars continued, "I will observe him and act as though I am not seen. Should he look at me, I will make sure not to look at him. Not too many of my kind are fond of making any sort of contact with the living."

"And should he try to challenge you?" Ezra asked.

"Do you want him alive?" Lars asked in response.

Ezra considered the question for a moment before he nodded. "Yes, yes, I suppose I do. Keep him alive. Incapacitate him if you must, but then come and inform me straight away. I do have physical, living assets available should I need them. And this man is presenting me with rather interesting challenges. I'd like to exact as much information from him as possible before I get rid of him."

"One last question, Mr. Pettigrew," Lars began. "What should happen if he sends me away as he did the others? Do I try again?"

Ezra shook his head. "I don't want to risk losing you to him."

Lars raised an eyebrow.

"It only makes sense that if he knows about ghosts," Ezra stated, "he would also know how to imprison them. I do not want to lose you, Lars. I expect great things from you."

The dead man straightened with pride. "Your confidence is well placed, Mr. Pettigrew. I will do great things. Now, where was this man last seen?"

"At the diner on Main Street," Ezra answered. "I'll point it out to you and then leave you to it. I have a suspicion he'll return sooner rather than later."

"Fair enough," Lars grinned. "Now what, Mr. Pettigrew?"

"Well, I'm planning on sending Theo out to cause a ruckus. It seems as though some of my workers aren't getting the hint. They're still causing a problem." Ezra took out a tiny bag, removed Lars' lock of hair from his pocket and nodded farewell before dropping the hair into the bag. As Ezra closed and sealed it, the dead man vanished, leaving Ezra alone on the bench. He slipped the bag back into his pocket and considered where to put Theo.

First, though, he needed to call James. He had not heard from the man since the day before, and considering the guidance the man needed of late, this was unusual.

Ezra extracted his phone from the Faraday bag, powered it up, and called James.

It rang five times and went to voice mail. Ezra didn't bother leaving a message. The sight of his number on James' missed calls list would be enough to make the man call back.

Ezra put his phone away, stood and headed back to his hotel.

"What's his name?" Theo asked.

"Will Mote," Ezra answered. "According to my information, he is personally responsible for the mechanical breakdown of two machines on the third shift. They were repaired by second shift the next day, but that is an unacceptable amount of downtime. And, the mechanic's report on the machines stated that the equipment had been sabotaged."

"That's a hell of a thing to do," Theo grumbled.

"Especially when it costs me money," Ezra agreed. "Not only the repairs, but to the lost production time as well."

"Still, what kind of rat does that?" The dead man shook his head. "Doesn't make sense. Not to me, anyway."

"We are in agreement there."

"What does he look like?" Theo asked.

Ezra took out a company ID photo and showed the dead man. Theo squinted at the image. "How tall?"

"Six foot two," Ezra answered. "Roughly one hundred eighty pounds. Smoker, drinker, and gambler, if the rumors among the employees are true. My sources say that Will sabotaged the machines so he could make some bets that had to be timed just right."

"What do you want done to him?"

Ezra had thought that out earlier.

"It is an easy solution," Ezra smiled. "Mr. Mote's position on the line is that of emergency stoppage. His sole task is to make certain nothing malformed enters the machine. He does not even need to use his hands, for there is an emergency shut-off button that is used by someone's feet. Hands would be necessary for quick responses after the shutdown of the machine. I believe that if his wrists are broken, he will still be able to stop the machine, if needed, and still be able to work, if only on light duty. It will save us some money and, I hope, teach the little weasel a valuable lesson."

"What lesson is that?" Theo asked.

"Don't break my equipment," Ezra answered. "Do not cost me money."

Theo chuckled. "Nice. Do you want him to see me when I do it?"

Ezra reflected on the effect Hyacinth's invisible assault had on Finn Reddington.

"No," Ezra told him. "I want you to stay hidden for as long as possible. Perhaps, in the end, you might show yourself. A bit of horror to drive the point home. What do you think?"

"It'll be more than a bit," Theo said with his mutilated grin. "I know what I look like, Mr. Pettigrew. Never looked like Clark Gable before I got killed, and I sure as hell don't look like him now."

"Fair enough," Ezra nodded. "Come now. I'll drop you off near Will's home, and then I will drop Lars near his task."

"Think that big old Swede is up to the task?"

"I do," Ezra confirmed. "I think you all are doing quite well. I am pleased with all of you. My hope is that this good luck will continue."

"You think it's luck?" Theo asked.

"Luck is always a part of it," Ezra nodded. "If it were simply a matter of letting you get about your business, there wouldn't be any doubt at all. But luck is a factor, and so we must prepare for something to go wrong."

"If you say so, Mr. Pettigrew. You're the boss."

"I am," Ezra agreed. "And I have been for a long time."

✳ ✳ ✳

Alice brought Stan a large chocolate pudding with a massive dollop of whipped cream atop it.

Stan looked up in surprise.

"Clyde Corville's mother heard about what you did," Alice explained. "She made you this and dropped it off here. She knows you don't eat up at Marilyn's unless the weather's bad enough for Mack to close the diner."

"Oh," Stan replied. "Will you please tell her I said thank you?"

"I already have," Alice replied with a wink. Then, a more serious expression filled her face. "Stan, you seem a little off today. Are you okay?"

"I am not," Stan answered. "I had a difficult evening. Far too many memories were brought up."

"I'm sorry," Alice told him. "Iraq?"

"Some of it."

"My grandfather was like that with Vietnam," Alice confided. "Sometimes, he'd disappear for days on a drinking spree. My grandmother said it was the only way he could deal with some of the things he saw."

"I understand that completely," Stan said.

"Well, I hope tonight's better." Alice patted him on the shoulder. "Now, you enjoy that pudding and call for more if you like. She must have brought over five gallons of it."

Stan lifted his spoon and dug into the pudding. Chocolate was his favorite, especially when whipped cream was added to it. He would not, however, ask for seconds. If he did, it would only lead to thirds, which, in turn, would result in a terrible stomachache.

With that in mind, Stan took his time, savoring each spoonful and doing his best not to think about the situation with Kenny, or what he had done to James Beckinsale.

As he ate the last of his dessert, Stan had the distinct sensation of being watched.

Lifting his head, he picked up his napkin, wiped carefully at his mouth and kept his head firmly fixed straight ahead. At the same time, he let his gaze drift to the window, where he saw a large ghost standing on the sidewalk and looking in.

Looking in and staring at Stan.

It was unusual enough to almost cause Stan to look out the window, but he fought back the urge. There had been too many ghosts in Mason as of late, and Stan suspected they were the work of Ezra Pettigrew. It was the only conclusion he could come up with.

Ezra Pettigrew had purchased the factory and changed the working conditions there.

James Beckinsale had told Stan that he reported directly to Ezra and that the problem of Kenny had been solved once he had done so.

More than that, Stan knew every ghost in Mason, and he walked through the town at least once a week to see if anyone new had drifted in, anchored to some item purchased over the week before.

In the past six months, there had only been one such individual, a young Frenchman who spoke no English and was quite content to sit in the yard of Mr. Abelard and listen to the birds.

With Mr. Pettigrew, however, there had been at least three ghosts, and now, a fourth standing and staring in at Stan. Staring into a place where Stan had stopped another attempted assault on factory employees.

Stan had no doubt the dead man on the sidewalk was watching him.

"You took a lot longer than I expected with that pudding," Alice said, smiling down at him as she approached the table.

He returned the smile and nodded. "Yes. I savored it."

"Would you care for another serving?"

"No, thank you. I would like a cup of tea please."

She raised an eyebrow. "Will wonders never cease? You've gone and done something different, Stan."

"Just this once," he told her. "I think it will help keep my stomach in order as I walk home."

"I'll be right back with it." Alice hurried off, shaking her head as she did so. When she entered the kitchen, he could hear her tell Mack about the tea.

Smiling, Stan turned his head to look out the window and past the ghost.

It was a test, really, to see how well the ghost might play the game of watch and wait.

He didn't play it well.

The ghost flinched as Stan looked toward him, then relaxed as he realized he was not the target of Stan's observation. Had the ghost really just been standing on the sidewalk, staring into the diner for whatever unfathomable reason, then he wouldn't have responded to Stan in the least.

That flinch, that slight movement around the eyes and the flare of the nostrils had told Stan everything he needed to know.

The dead man was there for him.

What the ghost intended to do, or how he intended to do it, Stan had no idea.

But he could work that out over tea, as he often did.

CHAPTER 35
COMPANY MAN

Will Mote finished his beer, set the can on the coffee table amongst the others, and lit up a fresh cigarette. The menthol sting of the Newports he favored brought tears to the corners of his eyes, and he wondered, idly, if there might ever be a time when he got used to that initial sting.

Running his free hand through his dirty hair, Will tried to remember when the game was going to be on. It didn't matter, not really. He'd forgotten to go to Manchester and put money down, so the game was a loss either way. He sure as hell didn't want to watch it and see his team win when he didn't have anything riding on it.

That would just make him mad.

He tapped the head off the cigarette into the newest empty beer can, then rummaged around the pocket attached to his easy chair until he found half a bag of sunflower seeds. Will pulled it out, took another long drag off the cigarette and then shook some of the seeds onto his lap.

He sat and smoked, ate the seeds and spat the shells onto the table.

Well, *most* of the shells onto the table.

It wasn't something he had to worry about, though. Ginger had moved out the week before. She had said she was tired of cleaning up after him and that there was no place to hide from his messes in the studio apartment.

"Whatever," Will muttered. She had gone running back to her parents' house up off of D Street. She could live there until she didn't want to deal with them, then she'd come crawling back.

Until then, Will wasn't going to clean a damned thing. That had been her job, and it was still going to be her job when she came back.

Or until he hooked up with someone else and had to make the damned place look respectable. At least for a little bit.

Will looked at the apartment and shook his head.

"She could have cleaned it before she left," he grumbled and then passed gas hard enough that he thought he had misjudged. Will sat for a moment, gauging the warmth in his undergarments.

Did he need to get up and shower?

He knew he needed to at some point but questioned whether that little bit of bodily action in his pants made it an immediate necessity.

With a shrug, he leaned over, opened the camping cooler by his chair's side, and removed another can of beer from the slowly melting ice. He did a quick count of the cooler's contents, saw he had another eleven beers left, and decided he would clean himself when the beers were finished.

Which meant he might have to take a day of sick leave from the factory.

Will grinned at the thought, popped the beer open, and took a long drink. He paused for a breath, belched, and drank again.

"Not too fast," he chided himself.

Will snorted a laugh and shook his head. He didn't know when he'd started talking to himself on a regular basis, but it'd been another complaint that Ginger had voiced.

Will frowned. The one before her had complained about it, too.

He shrugged and took another drink.

Will dug around the edges of the chair's cushion until he found his cell phone. It flickered to life behind the cracked display screen, and he frowned at it. He couldn't remember when he'd broken it. He didn't doubt he had done it, he was just frustrated he couldn't recall how. Usually, he remembered something like that.

Usually.

He tapped the passcode, brought up the call app and the phone died.

Will frowned, pressed the start button on the side and shook the phone several times, which occasionally worked when it was being difficult.

The trick didn't work, and the phone didn't power back up.

Will shivered at the sudden chill in the room and was surprised to see his own breath form into fog in front of him. He listened for the air conditioner, wondering if he had set the timer for it, but he didn't hear a thing. Not even the sound of the mini-fridge or the hum of the broken kitchen light.

He realized as he sat there, beer in one hand and phone in the other, that the lights had gone dead.

Will knew it wasn't his bills. He'd paid them. He always did.

This was something else. Something stranger, and for the first time, he understood he had drunk too much.

The hairs on his arms stood up, and his breath came out in quick gasps as he managed to push himself into a standing position. Fear built within him as he looked around for his wallet and car keys. He needed to get away from the building. The sooner, the better, and that primal knowledge continued to build as he shoved empty cans off the coffee table.

Will found his wallet, but the keys eluded him.

He knocked over a few more empty cans, and a voice screamed in him, *Run!*

Will turned and bolted for the door.

An unseen hand caught him in the right shoulder, spinning him around and sending him crashing over his chair and onto the floor. Something heavy slammed into his stomach, and he soiled himself fully.

With soaking clothing, he rolled onto his stomach and crawled toward the far window, which gave access to the fire escape.

"Where do you think you're going?" a voice asked, and a cold hand wrapped itself around his left ankle.

Will clawed at the rug as he was dragged backward, then thrown into the chair. He sat stiff and terrified, unable to move, his heart thundering against his chest.

"You're like a spider, I'll give you that," the unseen man said. "Quick as hell and probably just as dangerous if you can get a shot in. I don't have to worry about that, though. Am kind of upset. Know why?"

Will licked his lips and shook his head, trying to pinpoint the source of the voice in the darkness around him.

"'Cause I wasn't supposed to speak to you until the end, and I kind of lost my temper there, what with you crawling toward the window and all. Bet there's a fire escape out there, right?"

Will nodded.

"Yeah, can't have you getting out. Would kind of make it difficult to have our little conversation," the unseen man continued. "Difficult, but not impossible. I like it when things are easy, and you sure as hell aren't making them easy. You get me?"

Will nodded.

"Now, whether you'll believe it or not, I don't know, and hell, I don't care," the unseen speaker informed him, "I am here to correct you on your performance at work. You're screwing up, kid. Best way to say it."

Will felt cold sweat break out across the entirety of his body.

"Word is, you've got a gambling problem. Don't know if you play the dogs or the horses or if you just bet on the games, but you're making your problem your employer's problem. And your employer is not pleased. Fact is, Will," the unseen man's voice lowered to almost a whisper, "we know it was you who went and broke the machines."

Will's throat tightened. He wanted to try and deny it, but his instincts told him it would make the situation worse. The unseen man wasn't accusing Will, he was informing him.

And he didn't sound like a man who reacted well to being called a liar.

"You're not denying it?" the stranger asked.

Will could only shake his head.

"Damn, son," the stranger chuckled. "That's about the finest thing you could have done. I sure as hell wasn't expecting it. I want to thank you. You know, I was going to take my time with your punishment. I was even going to make it as bad as I could, but that was a stand-up thing you just did. I hope you understand that. Now, brace yourself, it won't be as bad as it would have been, but it sure as hell ain't going to be nice."

The stranger, Will learned, wasn't wrong.

CHAPTER 36
USEFUL INFORMATION

Ezra discovered it was better to meet with the dead outside.

In fact, he found that the local cemetery was the finest place to do so. Few people visited, and those who did were focused on their own grief and guilt.

Ezra, though, was concerned with neither.

Instead, he brought Lars' lock of hair in its container to the far left corner of the cemetery, where the woods crept up and into the wrought iron fence that wrapped the cemetery's borders. Ezra spread a towel from his hotel on the ground, sat down, and opened the container, freeing Lars.

The large man appeared a moment later, glancing at their surroundings.

A grin spread across his face.

"A good place you chose here," the dead man remarked as he sat down.

Ezra found it curious that the ghost did so, and he had to stop himself from asking if Lars could feel the grass beneath him.

"It is," Ezra agreed. "No one thinks twice about someone sitting alone and talking to a stone."

Lars laughed and nodded. "I suspect you'd like to know about our friend at the diner."

"I would. I would also like to know if he noticed you."

"From what I saw, he didn't," Lars said. "If he did, though, I'd hate to play poker against him."

Ezra frowned. "Yes. That would put a damper on things, wouldn't it?

Anyway, did you happen to find out who he is?"

"His name is Stan Owens," Lars stated. "He's known about town from what I gathered."

"Did you follow him?"

"All day until you picked me up," Lars nodded. "Like I said, he's known. Just about everywhere he went, someone wanted to talk to him. Cops, young and old people, pretty sure there was even a streetwalker who he had a chat with."

"Did you learn why?"

Lars shook his head. "Almost felt like he's a celebrity, you know? Everyone who knew him stopped to say hello. He wasn't out looking for it, either. Guy was just walking. But everywhere, and I mean everywhere, Mr. Pettigrew, people knew him. Hell, even a couple of cars pulled over to chat him up. Strange."

"Hmm," Ezra rubbed the back of his head. "Curious. Where does he work?"

"Doesn't. Not that I could see," Lars said, shrugging. "Ate his lunch at the diner. Ate his dinner at the diner. Stopped in between the two for a cup of tea at the diner. Seems like he takes most meals there. They didn't bring him a menu, just a meal. My guess is he's got a set routine."

Ezra frowned. "Where does he live?"

"Rooming house," Lars answered. "Went back before dark. Place is run by an older lady, and they seem pretty chummy."

Ezra raised an eyebrow. "Really?"

"Not like they're an item or anything," Lars clarified. "No. More like they've known each other for a hell of a long time. Might have been something before, but not now, you know?"

"No," Ezra confessed. "But go on, please."

"Not much more to go on about," Lars said. "He had another cup of tea, you'd think the guy was a Brit the way he puts it away, and read a book for a while before he went on up to bed."

"What was in his room?" Ezra asked. "Pictures of family? Anything at all?"

"Nothing." Lars frowned. "Strange, really. Clothes in his closet. A bed, a small chair and a bed table with a lamp on it. Oh, an alarm clock, too. Bed was all made up. Sharp hospital corners like you'd find in, well, a hospital or a prison. Guy's regimented. Kind of reminds me of a few guys I knew who did time."

"What do you mean by 'did time'?" Ezra asked.

"Prison time," Lars explained. "Not jail time, prison time. I'm thinking five years at least. Probably closer to ten."

"This is all excellent information," Ezra sighed. "I have to think of how to apply it now. Is he a reformed prisoner? If so, why is he so well-liked in town? What has he to do with the factory?"

"You'll check to see if he's on the roll?"

"Hmm? Oh, yes, I certainly will," Ezra nodded. "I've been trying to reach James, the factory's manager, and I've had no success. It is unusual for him to be silent. He is an exceptionally receptive subordinate."

Lars frowned, and Ezra smiled.

"He's a good worker," Ezra clarified.

"You think something bad happened to him?"

Ezra started to shake his head, then stopped. "I don't know. I should check on him."

"Sounds like a good idea, Mr. Pettigrew," Lars agreed. "I'll step away, and you can give me a holler when you're done."

The dead man faded, and Ezra removed his phone from the Faraday bag. He turned on his phone and waited to see if there were any messages from James.

There weren't.

He called James and it went straight to voicemail.

With a growing sense of anxiety, Ezra sent the man a simple text. *Call me.*

If something had happened to James, the entire plan regarding the factory would be in danger. And that would mean a loss of profits.

Besides, Ezra needed James to be the fall guy, should the situation warrant it. Replacing the man at this point in the endeavor would be difficult and frustrating, to say the least.

With a shake of his head, Ezra powered down his phone returned it to the Faraday bag and called out for Lars. He needed to get the dead man back to the suite, and then Ezra had to confirm with Theo that the situation with the gambling employee had been taken care of.

Ezra had a great deal to do and a shrinking amount of time to do it.

CHAPTER 37

EDUCATION AND ASSISTANCE

The dead man had followed Stan the remainder of the previous day, and Stan had kept to his normal routine.

The morning had been free of the ghost, as had the afternoon, and the evening was looking the same. That pleased Stan, for he knew he needed help and that the only one who could help him would be Adam.

The young man had proven himself courageous and capable in the past, and now it was time to see if he could go further. Could he take a step toward fighting the dead?

It was a difficult question and one he had hesitated to ask Adam. Stan had mentioned it in passing, brought him along on some of the easier situations, but had not wanted to broach the subject completely.

But now there was no choice.

The dead man who had followed him had shown Stan that.

The death of Kenny had shown him that.

"Would you like another cup of tea?" Marilyn asked.

Stan blinked, looked up and shook his head. "No, thank you, Marilyn."

The front door opened, and he heard the familiar tread of Adam, then the young man's voice as he greeted Marilyn.

"Good evening, Adam," she smiled, stepping out of the doorway to allow him to pass through.

The young man's face was flush, and he had a broad grin on his face.

"Were you out with Agatha?" Marilyn asked, and Adam's cheeks became a deeper shade of red. "Good for you. She comes from a good family."

Marilyn left the room, and Adam looked at Stan. "Everything okay?"

"No," Stan replied. "There is something I need to speak with you about."

"Oh." Adam sat down. He was about to speak again when his phone chimed. Stan waited as Adam retrieved it, looked at the message and typed in a quick response.

"That was Sheriff Bowman," Adam said. "He said another worker from the factory was injured. Two broken wrists with some frostbite to the skin. Guy won't say how the breaks happened."

Stan frowned. "This is what I wished to speak to you about."

"The attacks?"

Stan nodded.

"You know I want to help you," Adam told him. "You've got me learning how to make boxes to keep ghosts locked up, and that's great. But I want to know how to put them in there, Stan. You've helped me more than I can say. Hell, all of Mason has helped me. This place has picked me up and put me back together. I feel like a man for the first time in my life. I can walk down Main Street, and people greet me. They don't turn their eyes away. They don't ignore me. Hell, Stan, I've got a beautiful girl who likes to spend time with me. Tell me what I need to do to help you and to help this town."

"Catching ghosts can be both difficult and dangerous, as you can see by those who have been attacked by them," Stan replied. "We have buried three people because of the dead. There are ways to protect yourself from them, but those ways are not foolproof."

"How do you do it?" Adam asked. "You never really told me. You said it had something to do with iron and kind of left it at that."

"It does," Stan answered and then paused a moment before adding, "and I shall leave it at that for myself. For you, my friend, we will need to equip you with iron if you are amicable to the idea."

"I am, Stan," Adam answered. "Like I said, I want to help."

Stan nodded. "It will be dangerous."

"That's fine."

Stan reached into his vest pocket and removed a small, thin envelope. "I apologize for the rough design. We can fine-tune them later, make them more comfortable."

Stan opened the envelope and slid out a pair of rings. The rings were not completed, for each of them had a slight gap. He passed them to Adam, who accepted them and managed to slide one on each index finger.

"They're a little tight," Adam observed, flexing his fingers. "Not too bad, though. I think if I get a pair of pliers, I might be able to make them a little more comfortable. What are they made out of?"

"Iron coffin nails," Stan told him.

Adam looked surprised. "You bought coffin nails just to make these?"

Stan shook his head. "No. Some years ago, one of the older cemeteries in Plaistow, New Hampshire, was moved, and more than a few of the coffins fell apart. I gathered up the nails I could find."

Stan heard the dry click of Adam's throat as the younger man swallowed.

"You must wear those rings whenever we engage the dead," Stan informed him. "I do not know the reason why, but when iron comes into contact with a ghost, it sends the ghost back to the item it possesses or haunts. When surrounded by iron, a ghost can be contained. This is why the older cemeteries are fenced in by wrought iron. It is to keep the dead in."

"You're joking, right?" Adam asked.

Stan frowned. "Why would I be? Our ancestors were not fools, Adam. Being able to see the dead is not something new. It is a trait that people have had throughout history. I am, in no way, unique in this regard. It should come as no surprise that New Englanders knew to take no chances. Iron fencing was a simple, elegant solution to a possibly dangerous problem. The containment function is excellent, but it is the casting away aspect which is most beneficial to us."

"And that's what these will do?" Adam asked, holding his hands up and looking at the rings.

"So long as you put them through a ghost, yes."

Adam raised an eyebrow.

"The iron must make contact with the ghost," Stan confirmed. "Your best option is to make sure that occurs."

"Got it. Punch ghosts with iron fists."

Stan nodded. "Yes."

"Okay. What about salt and lead?" Adam asked.

"While salt and lead do not cast the dead back to their items," Stan explained, "they do serve as containers. If you place salt across thresholds or windowsills, you will keep the dead out of a room. Should a ghost be in the room, those items will keep the ghost there. I have heard of larger rooms that have been lined in lead, but that is a great amount of work for little return, as far as I am concerned. Lead is exceptionally useful regarding small containment. That is why I prefer to use it as a liner in the boxes I create. When properly formed, lead will keep a ghost in place indefinitely."

"Got it." Adam paused, then asked, "Are ghosts always attached to small items?"

Stan shook his head.

"No? Are we talking big like, I don't know, a car?"

"An entire building can be a haunted item," Stan explained. "When that occurs, it takes a great deal of work to create a barrier which prohibits the ghost from moving from the property."

Adam frowned, confused. "Wait a minute. How far can a ghost move? I mean, do they go on trips?"

"From what I have read," Stan stated, "spirits can travel up to a mile from their objects."

Adam didn't respond for a moment.

"A mile? From their object?"

"Yes."

"So, a mile radius?"

"Yes," Stan said again.

"Wow." Adam cleared his throat. "That's a lot of room to move around in."

"It is," Stan agreed. "This places us at a significant disadvantage."

"Does this have anything to do with the size of the ghost's object?" Adam asked. "I mean, if they're haunting a comb or something, does that lessen the distance they can travel?"

"No, not at all. The size of the object has nothing to do with it." Stan shrugged. "It really is a curious aspect of the dead. This is why we must carry the boxes with us. We must be prepared to take a ghost's object and contain it whenever necessary."

"Great," Adam muttered. "Can we *kill* a ghost? Is that even the right term to use?"

"It is not, but there is a theory that a ghost can be destroyed."

"How does that work?"

"We would need to obtain the object the ghost is attached to," Stan said. "And then, we would need to destroy it."

"That's it?"

"Well, according to the one source who has given me this information," Stan continued, "there is a significant chance that we would be injured should we take this route."

"Why's that?" Adam asked.

"According to her, the object explodes. Again, the intensity of the explosion will more than likely be in direct correlation to the power of the ghost we are seeking to destroy. We might be injured or killed in the resulting destruction of the object."

"Yeah," Adam sighed. "That would definitely be pretty terrible. Anything else?"

Stan frowned. "I am sure there is, but I cannot remember at this time. Are you sure you still want to do this, Adam?"

Adam grinned, flexed his hands once more and nodded.

"Yeah, you're damned right I do."

CHAPTER 38
A WORD WITH JAMES

Ezra didn't bring any of the dead with him when he went to check on James.

James Beckinsale seemed frightened of his own shadow at times, and Ezra hoped that the attacks on the recalcitrant employees hadn't made the man doubt the necessary tactics. Beckinsale had little backbone as it was. Fear might turn him into a jellyfish.

Ezra chuckled at the image of a spineless James Beckinsale as he climbed up the few steps to the small house purchased for factory management. He rang the doorbell, and when James didn't respond within a minute, Ezra rapped on the door several times.

A faint creak reached his ears, and then, from the other side of the door, came James' voice.

"Who is it?"

Fear and caution filled the words, and the recognition of them brought a frown to Ezra's face.

"Damn it, James, it's Ezra. Open the door!"

A chain rattled and the deadbolt clicked a heartbeat later, and then the door was tugged open.

Without waiting, Ezra pushed his way in, turned sharply around and opened his mouth to berate James. The words died in his mouth when he looked at the man.

His face was pale, his hair white, and he stared with terror.

Ezra closed the door. "What happened to you?"

James licked his lips, glanced around, and whispered, "I was tortured."

For the first time, Ezra realized all the lights were on in the house. "How?" he asked.

"A man broke in," James answered, limping to the couch and sitting down, wincing as he did so. "He asked me questions and hurt me until I answered them."

Ezra brought a chair close to the couch and sat down. "What sort of questions?"

"He wanted to know who owned the factory." James' voice was barely audible.

"Did you tell him?"

James nodded. "I tried not to. I really did. But he hurt me, Mr. Pettigrew. For a long, long time."

Ezra looked at James and felt neither anger nor disappointment. How could he? He had hired the man to run a factory, not withstand torture.

"What else did he ask you?" Ezra kept his tone gentle.

"He wanted to know why Kenny had been killed," James answered. "He wanted to know why ghosts were around the factory."

"Did you tell him anything about Kenny?"

James nodded. "That he was trouble. I was sorry he had died, but the man was trouble."

"What did he do then?"

"He told me Kenny was his friend," James replied.

"And did he torture you more after that?"

James shook his head. "He knew it wasn't my fault, he said. And when I told him I really didn't know anything about the ghosts, he said he believed me."

Ezra rubbed the back of his head for a moment. "James, could you talk to a sketch artist if I brought one in? So we can find out who it is?"

"I know who it is, Mr. Pettigrew," James said, his voice hushed. "He told me his name."

Ezra blinked. "What is it?"

"Stanley Owens," James whispered. "And he said he's coming for you."

✳ ✳ ✳

A private ambulance left the house, taking James Beckinsale with it.

Ezra remained behind. He would have someone come in and pack up James' belongings and have them sent along. Despite James' weaknesses when it came to properly running a factory, the man was impressively loyal. Ezra would reward that.

Once the situation with the factory and Stan Owens was resolved, and not until then.

But James most certainly deserved it.

"And what do I deserve?" Ezra asked himself softly.

"Everything," he stated a moment later. "This is nothing more than a hiccup here. I will remove Stanley Owens. I will have my factory and the money coming to me. It is as simple as that. And, as my father always said, keep it simple."

Ezra closed the door, locked it and left the building for his car.

It was time to deal with Stan Owens before the man became more of a problem.

✳ ✳ ✳

Darryl Rarest rubbed at his nose and frowned. "So, I'm supposed to go after another one of these guys for you?"

Ezra didn't let his frustration show. "Yes. His name is Finn Reddington. Hyacinth already dealt with him, but I would like the message to be reiterated."

"You want me to beat him a bit more?"

"No," Ezra answered, shaking his head. "I want you to scare him. Remind him to behave."

"In his house?"

"Yes," Ezra smiled. "I'll place you close to it so you can operate freely."

"What if he's with somebody? You still want me to go at him?" Darryl asked.

"I most certainly do," Ezra confirmed. "He needs to be reminded, and whoever is with him will help him do so every time he looks at them. But remember, I do not want any physical contact. Do not damage anyone there. Is this understood?"

"Yup," Darryl nodded. "Look, but don't touch. What about if I run into that other guy? The one that screwed up the deal at the diner?"

"Should that happen, get to your item and remain still," Ezra ordered. "I will collect you as soon as possible."

"Okay," Darryl grinned. "Let's go meet Finn."

CHAPTER 39

AN UNWANTED GUEST

Finn sat in his backyard, the afternoon light fully upon the man.

Adam sat across from him, waiting for Finn to answer the question.

"I don't know," Finn finally answered, his voice rough. He shifted his gaze to Adam. "Wish to hell I had seen something, but honestly, Adam, I was getting the beat down of my life in that bathroom. I wasn't looking for anything but a way out."

"I understand," Adam replied.

Finn adjusted his position in the chair. "Stan was coming, right? Didn't you say that?"

"Yes," Adam nodded. "He'll be here. He had to talk to Marilyn about something first, but he'll be here soon."

"That's good," Finn sighed, and his shoulders relaxed. "I trust that man with my life."

Adam hesitated, then asked, "Why is that?"

Finn looked at him in surprise. "You don't know?"

"No."

"Huh," Finn muttered. In a slightly louder voice, he continued, "Just about everybody in Mason owes Stan Owens something, Adam. He's helped out folks for as long as I can remember."

"With ghosts?" Adam asked, surprised.

A grim smile spread across Finn's face. "Oh yes. With ghosts. I don't know if ghosts are as much of a problem in other towns, but Mason's had a hell of a lot of them over the years. Most of it started back in 2005 when the old Kennedy House caught fire. Place collapsed in on itself and the firefighters put it out. But the electrical system went with it, and Stan said that was the real problem. That and the looters that broke into the bomb shelter that Mrs. Kennedy had built under her greenhouse. With no power, well, there was nothing to keep the door locked once the looters got through the mechanical locks. Mrs. Kennedy collected haunted antiques, if you can believe it. Stan said something about the seals being broken and that let the ghosts go. Then, you had the fact that the looters set up shop at the Hollis Flea Market and sold those stolen goods for a song and a dance. A hell of a lot of them ended up back here, for some reason, and for years, there was hell to pay."

"That bad?" Adam asked.

Finn nodded. "Take a walk through Carpenter's Cemetery sometime. There's a whole lot of headstones from 2005 to 2008. It took Stan working every day for almost three years to get the mess cleaned up. And he did it for free."

The two men were silent for a short time. Finally, Finn broke it. "He never talks about it?"

"No," Adam answered. "He doesn't talk about a whole lot. Not really. I kind of wonder what he was like when he was younger. You heard about the fight at Dow's recently?"

"Bits and pieces," Finn said. "You were there, right?"

"Yeah." Adam cleared his throat. "I've seen some street fights. You know, when I was on the street for a while. Bad fights, but nothing like what I saw at Dow's. His fight made me think of those action movies I used to love as a kid. Except Stan was faster. A lot faster."

"You wouldn't expect it," Finn said. "Not with the way he looks. Or the way he talks."

Adam nodded in agreement.

"You can't judge a book by its cover."

Adam looked over his shoulder, and Rita, Finn's wife, came walking down the back steps. She winced as she did so, one hand under her large belly.

"How are you two doing?" Finn asked, shifting his attention to her.

"Well, she's beating the hell out of my kidneys," Rita muttered, sitting down in a lawn chair beside her husband. "Two months to go, and I swear this kid wants to come out now. I blame you for all of this, Finn."

"I know you do, Sweetheart," the man smiled.

Rita turned toward Adam, brushed a strand of curly red hair out of her eyes and sighed. "I know a bit about Stan and the Owens family."

Both Adam and Finn looked at her.

"My mom's his distant cousin," Rita explained. "She always said that that side of the family was a little rough. I found out later on just how rough. Apparently, Stan's granduncle used to be a heavy for folks in Manchester. He would take Stan with him since Stan and his sisters lived with him and his wife. According to my mom, Stan was told he had to earn his and his sisters' keep. It's how he learned to fight."

"When did that start?" Finn asked.

"My mom never said," Rita answered. "But I get the idea it was pretty early on in his life. Both his parents died, although I don't know how. His sisters were younger than him."

"Do his sisters still live in Mason?" Adam asked.

"I don't even know if they're alive," Rita said. "I think only Marilyn would know. She was pretty close with their mother."

"I heard he was friends with her son. Makes sense he's staying with her now. He's like a son to her," Adam said.

"Their house is still there, you know," Rita remarked. "The house he grew up in?"

Adam's eyes widened. "What?"

"Yeah," Rita continued. "It's been in the family for a few generations. In fact, that's where his granduncle and grandaunt died. Granduncle had a heart attack right after he murdered his wife."

"My story is an old one," Stan said as he stepped around the building.

Stan had heard Rita speaking as he walked along toward the back of the house, and he did not slow as he heard what she was saying.

Why should he? He knew his own history, and he did not attempt to hide it. Kenny had helped him understand he did not need to hide his past, had helped him realize that he did not need to be ashamed of what had made him who he was.

The three sat in silence, and Stan did his best to set them at ease.

"I take no offense at my story being discussed, Rita," Stan stated. "It is common knowledge. For the most part."

"I'm sorry, Stan," she said, twisting her hands together nervously.

"There is no need to apologize, although I do appreciate the thought," he informed her. "I tend not to speak of it because, well, I do not speak of many things."

Finn let out a nervous chuckle and nodded.

Adam's face was bright red, as though he was a child caught in a lie.

Stan found a folded lawn chair, unfolded it, undid the button on his suit coat, and sat down.

"My young friends," he began, "my history is one of violence. Today is not the day for details, but I will give you the very basics. My parents were murdered when I was young. My relatives were abusive toward me, although they did care for my sisters, which is all that mattered. I learned how to fight and how to not care about who I hurt or why I had to hurt them. It did not bother me when my granduncle smothered my grandaunt in their bed or when I found them both that evening. I joined the Army and sent my money home to my sisters. When they graduated high school, they left Mason, and I have not heard from them since. I do not blame them. My blame, for many years, was reserved for myself."

The three all looked at him, unsure of how to respond, and Stan forced himself to smile.

He was about to speak again when the same ghost he had stopped at the diner from harming the Corville cousins appeared.

"Adam?" Stan looked at the young man.

"Yes?"

"Do you have the box I asked you to bring?"

Adam patted his jacket pocket. "Yeah. Right here. Why?"

"We are going to need it. Go out to the front of the house and start looking for something that does not look right," Stan told him.

Before he could add anything else, the ghost launched himself toward Finn, and Stan sprang out of his own seat. He pulled Finn out of the way and slammed his fist into the oncoming ghost, biting back the sharp, cold pain of first contact with the dead man. The ghost vanished, leaving Stan alone with Finn and Rita, both of whom looked at him with frightened expressions.

"Rita," Stan said. "Go. Finn, you must stay with me."

Rita and Finn looked at each other, and then Finn nodded. As his wife hurried away, the man looked at Stan.

"Another ghost?" Finn asked, his voice tight and his face pinched with fear.

"Yes," Stan managed to say, and then the ghost was back.

The dead man looked at Stan warily, then picked up a lawn chair and hurled it at him, Finn letting out a gasp of fear.

Stan sidestepped the object and kept his eyes locked on the ghost.

"Get behind me, Finn," Stan ordered, and Finn did so.

"How the hell did you do that?" the dead man demanded.

Stan didn't respond, and the ghost threw another chair.

This one Stan caught, cast aside and asked, "Who are you?"

The ghost sneered at him. "You wanna trade names, huh? Get to know each other a little before I beat you and your friend to hell."

Stan was about to answer but stopped himself as the dead man bolted toward him. He didn't bother throwing a punch. He merely stepped in the way and let the ghost barrel into him. His heart skipped a beat with the shock of the cold, and the dead man was gone a second later.

"I can't see him," Finn whispered, and Stan heard the fear in the man's voice.

"All is well. We will stand firm."

"Is it going to come back?" Finn asked.

"He's already here," Stan answered as the dead man reappeared.

Adam's heart thumped wildly against his chest, terror threatening to engulf him as he looked around. He tried to spot anything out of place, anything that might be a haunted object, such as Stan had spoken of.

Even as he searched, the remembered fear of the dead from his past climbed up from the shadows of his memories, and he shoved them back.

As the last memory vanished, he heard a soft crack, and when he looked for the source of the noise, he saw a bit of grass, brittle in the light. In the center of the frozen vegetation, Adam saw a tooth. An old, yellowed human tooth with a cracked filling. It took only a moment for him to see it for what it was, and he fumbled in his jacket for the lead-lined box.

Adam dropped to his knees, opened the box and, ignoring the stinging pain of the frozen tooth against his fingertips, snatched the tooth from the ground.

"I'm going to kill you," the dead man snarled, crouching down and lifting a fist-sized stone.

Stan could see the effort it took the dead man, the immense amount of stress placed on the ghost.

But still, the dead man lifted the stone, raised it above his head and then vanished.

The stone fell with a thud and rolled a few inches toward Stan.

Adam came running around the side of the building, his face pale and beaded with sweat. He held a lead-lined box aloft, and a victorious grin spread appeared.

"Got him!" Adam exclaimed. "We got him!"

Finn collapsed into a sitting position on the ground.

"Excellent," Stan nodded. "Let us take him back to the barn. There's a room there where we will not need to fear any interruptions."

CHAPTER 40
DIRECT METHODS

Ezra watched as Finn Reddington and his wife got into their pickup truck and left their home.

The man was not injured.

The Reddingtons looked terrified, which was pleasing, but the man had not been harmed. And that had been the entire point of the exercise. Strike additional fear into him, and thus the workers, as well as possibly drawing out Stan Owens.

The effort, it appeared, had failed spectacularly, and Ezra wanted to know why.

Once the Reddingtons had turned off their street, Ezra stepped out of his car and strolled up the front of their house. He kept a neutral expression on his face as he moved along, hands in his pockets. When he reached the spot where he had left Darryl's tooth, he stopped and knelt as though to tie his shoe. He went to pick up the tooth and froze.

It wasn't there.

Ezra found frozen grass, something he had never seen with the others, but the tooth was gone. There weren't any fragments either. The tooth hadn't been destroyed.

Confused, Ezra stood up, turned and walked back to his car. He didn't bother with any pretense. Something had happened, and he was certain it wasn't good.

✳ ✳ ✳

Back at the hotel, Ezra sat in front of his computer. He had pulled up the Roys' website and looked at the blank fields for the Contact Us form. His eyes focused on the "Usually answers in an hour" statement at the bottom.

Ezra waited only a moment longer, then typed in his false information with a newly created email, followed by his question.

Hello, I had a ghost object that I left outside (kind of worried about it). When I went back this morning, there was frozen grass. No sign of the object, though. No bits or pieces. Could something make a ghost object disappear? Thanks.

Ezra looked at what he had written, made certain it said exactly what he wanted it to, and then hit send.

He stood up, went into his bedroom and pulled out Theo's object. Within a few seconds, the dead man was there.

"Hey, Boss," Theo greeted, then he frowned. "What's going on?"

"One of the objects has vanished," Ezra stated.

"How?"

"I don't know." Ezra explained what he had set Darryl out to do and what he had found on his return.

"That *is* baffling," Theo said when Ezra finished. "I don't know a whole lot to begin with, but that sure as hell don't sound right."

"No," Ezra agreed. "I didn't think it sounded right either."

"There any way you can find out?"

Ezra nodded. "Well, I hope so. I've left a message for some experts. I'm hoping they can offer some sort of information for me."

"What if it's bad news?" Theo asked.

Ezra gave the dead man a cold grin. "That is, unfortunately, exactly what I am expecting at this point, Theo. Right now, I am hopeful there will be some good news. But it is as they say, hope for the best, prepare for the worst."

"And how are you gonna prepare for the worst?" the ghost inquired.

"First, we need to discuss where to strike to exert some sort of control over the town."

Theo grinned. "Gonna attack the place?"

"Yes. That is exactly what we're going to do," Ezra confirmed.

"That ought to be fantastic," the ghost chuckled. "We going to kill?"

"Yes," Ezra replied, keeping his tone measured.

He was concerned about more deaths. Not from any moral objection to it but because death generally brought out investigators, and he didn't want any of that. He had a tenuous grip on a few lines of communication into New Hampshire's law enforcement community, but he lacked the ability to strengthen it. Ezra, it turned out, was not the only man interested in unexplainable deaths, and it seemed most of that information was funneled to another individual. And all he had learned about that man was that the person in question resided in Nashua.

A person who had far more pull than Ezra did.

"Will it just be the two of us?" Theo asked.

"Hmm? Oh, no." Ezra shook his head. "It will be you, Hyacinth and Lars."

"Okay," Theo shrugged, but Ezra could see the dead man was displeased with the response.

He pushed Theo's reaction away. "You will attack at one point, and one point only. I believe that bringing an overwhelming force to bear on this place will, shall we say, prohibit further involvement from parties that are far too interested in what I'm doing."

Theo frowned, and Ezra refrained from sighing.

"We're going to hit the right person," Ezra explained. "With the right amount of force. When we're done, he won't be able to do anything again."

"Who's that?" Theo asked.

"A man named Stanley Owens," Ezra answered.

CHAPTER 41
AN UNINTERRUPTED INTERVIEW

"Do you need me in here?" Adam asked.

Stan shook his head. "No. Thank you, though. If you could go back into the house and ask Marilyn to put on a pot of tea, I would greatly appreciate it."

Stan watched as Adam nodded with some relief and then left the barn.

The young man was still fighting with his fear of the dead, and Stan found it admirable. There were some who never could have overcome their fear. In his life, Stan had known more than a few of them.

Letting those memories fade back into the recesses of his mind, he walked into the barn and to the small room that served as his ghostly penitentiary.

Like his familial home, the small room was secured by salt, with additional lines of iron embedded into the wood, walls and ceilings. Soft lights came from standing lamps set in the corner and from beside a tall, austere wooden chair. Beside the chair was a small, functional table and beyond that, open space. Shelves lined the walls of the room, and many of the shelves were occupied by anywhere from a dozen to three dozen leaden boxes.

Stan did not place too many boxes on the shelves. Too much weight would bring an entire set of shelves down, and that could prove dangerous.

Before sitting in his chair, he wandered the small room, making sure the iron inlay of the boards was still intact. The iron and the containers for the dead should keep the dead on the shelf should anything happen to its case. Stan did not want to risk a massive breakout, one that could unleash devastation on Marilyn and her tenants.

Satisfied the room was secure, he set the newest box on the floor, opened it, and sat in his chair.

The dead man he had struggled with appeared a moment later, head jerking from left to right as he tried to orient himself. Finally, he saw Stan and snarled.

"Hello," Stan greeted.

The dead man swore at him. Stan didn't react.

The ghost started toward him, paused, and then walked past, only to let out a pained gasp of surprise as he stopped at the door.

"Iron," Stan explained. "I am sorry to inform you that you cannot leave this room."

Cold struck the back of his head, and then the dead man reappeared by the box on the floor a moment later.

"How?" the dead man demanded.

"How what?" Stan countered.

"Why can't I touch you?!"

"You can," Stan replied. "However, I have been modified after a fashion. The dead find me difficult to physically interact with."

"That ain't an answer," the ghost snapped back.

"It is, it just is not the answer you want," Stan stated.

The dead man clenched his hands into fists and turned around, searching the room. After a moment, he faced Stan again. "How the hell do I get out of here?"

"You do not," Stan informed him. "This is where you will remain. Forever."

The ghost shook his head. "No. That ain't happening. I'm leaving. You're letting me out."

"No."

The dead man turned and tried to get to the window, but inlaid iron drove him back.

As he looked at Stan again, Stan saw desperate understanding filling the dead man's face.

"I can't stay here," the ghost hissed. "I got too much to do."

"You are dead, sir," Stan reminded him. "There is nothing you need to do other than move on to your just reward, although I suspect it will not be quite as you hoped for."

"I'm not going to tell you a damned thing," the dead man snapped.

Stan looked at him, saw the ghost was telling the truth, and sighed.

Without a word, Stan stood, crossed the room and ignored the shouts of the dead man. Instead, he focused on closing the lid on the box.

Silence returned a heartbeat later, and Stan placed the box on a shelf.

Ezra typed, *Thank you!*

With a frown, he hit the send button and then left the room, returning to where Theo waited.

The dead man raised an eyebrow in question.

"Apparently," Ezra began, sitting down, "the frozen patch means a great deal of energy was expended by the ghost. However, the item, in this case, Darryl's tooth, should have been there. This means someone took it."

"Who do you think took it?"

"It can only be Stan Owens," Ezra grumbled.

"What do you want to do about it?"

Ezra paused, then stated, "We're going to attack the place where he lives. Lars knows it. Apparently, Mr. Owens lives in a boarding house and is well-known amongst the tenants there. With any luck, you and the others should be able to terrorize the home and perhaps kill Mr. Owens."

Theo nodded. "What if we don't kill him?"

"Then injure, incapacitate. Put him in a damned hospital!"

Ezra cleared his throat and regained his composure.

"The point," he continued, "is to ensure he does not interfere with us again. I have a great deal of money invested in the factory here. Enough that to leave now would result in a financial loss I am unwilling to accept unless absolutely necessary."

"Okay. When do you want to hit the house?"

"Now," Ezra answered and got to his feet.

Adam climbed out of the shower, dried off and dressed quickly. In less than an hour he was meeting Agatha in Nashua for dinner, and he liked being early. As he stood in front of the mirror, adjusting the collar of his shirt and the line of his vest, he realized he was dressing more and more like Stan.

A smile passed his lips, and he chuckled. There were far worse people to imitate.

Satisfied that he looked presentable, Adam slipped his phone into his back pocket and then froze as a window shattered on the first floor.

Within the space of a breath, he regained his composure and threw open his door. His shoes thundered on the stairs as he raced down to the first floor and found himself facing the dead in the parlor.

Broken glass lay shattered on the floor and Marilyn was backed into a corner, an iron fireplace poker in her hand. Her face was set in a grim frown, and her eyes never left the trio of ghosts when she spoke to Adam.

"Do you have iron?" she asked him.

"I do," Adam answered and then realized he didn't.

The rings Stan had given him were upstairs in his room, waiting on his bed along with his watch and wallet.

He glanced at the dead.

A large blonde man who reminded Adam of a Viking, a small woman, and a man who looked like an extra out of a war movie, charred and mutilated, all stood menacingly in front of him.

Adam dove for the iron shovel by the fireplace as the ghosts attacked.

Ezra looked from the three items in the yard in front of him to the house. He had heard the window break, although he didn't know from what. From where he stood, he could not see into the house, but he heard the dead and the sound of their rampage, which made him smile.

Soon, he knew, they would return to him. Return and bring him joyous news of the death of Stan Owens. Or at least his injuring.

There could be no other outcome.

A grin spread across his face as he leaned against his rental and crossed his arms over his chest. As he did so, he let his gaze drift across the house, and then he stiffened.

Stan Owens walked around the side of the building and paused.

* * *

Stan heard the harsh noises of fighting and saw the stranger leaning against a vehicle parked where no one ever parked on the street. The man straightened up, and his head dipped for a moment. Stan followed the man's line of sight and saw a piece of cloth on the ground and unidentifiable objects upon it.

The stranger made a half step toward the cloth, and for the first time in years, Stan broke into a sprint.

* * *

Ezra could only describe the burst of speed from Stan Owens as maniacal, and that was in the split second it took him to realize what Owens was doing.

Fear took over, and Ezra stumbled forward. He scooped up the cloth on the ground, hastily bunched it up and staggered around to the other side of the vehicle. He fumbled in, locked the door, and glanced to the passenger side window in time to see Stan Owens cock his fist and launch it forward.

The tempered safety glass shattered, and by the time Stan withdrew his arm, Ezra had the engine started. From the corner of his eye, he saw the man trying to reach in and unlock the door.

With his breath caught in his throat, Ezra threw the vehicle into gear, stomped on the gas and jerked the car away from the curb. Stan fell back, and Ezra didn't bother looking in the mirrors.

The last thing he wanted to see was Stan Owens chasing after him.

Stan ignored his bleeding hand as he turned back to where the cloth had been.

Whoever had gotten away had been in a rush, and he had left a single item behind on the cracked sidewalk.

An old button emblazoned with an anchor.

It was cold to the touch, and without a word, Stan put the button into a lead-lined box.

With the object secure, he returned the box to his inner pocket and went up to the house to see what sort of damage had been done.

CHAPTER 42
TACTICAL RETREAT

Ezra stood in his suite of rooms, looking down at the pair of objects on the table. Lars' lock of hair and Hyacinth's ring with its broken setting.

Theo's button was missing.

Darryl was captured.

Within the space of hours, Ezra was down fifty percent of his active ghostly assets. He didn't include the two he had received previously from the store in his count. They still hadn't made an appearance, and he didn't believe they would any time soon.

In addition to the loss of Theo and Darryl, Ezra had suffered the loss of James Beckinsale. While the man was not particularly adept in this line of work, he had proven loyal, and Ezra had to repay that.

It was time to cut his losses with the factory. He would move James to a safe place and sell the facility. With any luck, he could recoup at least the money he had invested. If not, he would take the loss and move on to another target.

There were plenty for him to enjoy.

Before the dead could question why they were pulled from the house, Ezra put both items into a small, lined bag and tucked it away. He retrieved his phone from its Faraday bag and dialed his primary assistant.

"Sir?" Robert answered on the second ring.

"Hello, Robert," Ezra greeted. "I need Abigail to send a crew to pack up my things here. I also need a medical flight for James home and then a first-class flight for myself."

Ezra listened as Robert's pen scratched across the surface of a paper.

"Anything else, sir?" Robert asked after a moment.

"Yes," Ezra sighed. "I have to cut my losses with this facility. Please begin the process of selling it through the shell companies. There is a gentleman here who is not pleased with me. I'd rather he not have any sort of trail to follow."

"Of course, sir," Robert replied. "Would you like me to bring in Mr. Bikram?"

Ezra considered the suggestion, then nodded. "Yes. That's an excellent idea, Robert, thank you. Bring in Mr. Bikram and ask him to coordinate the sales and such. Offer him a bonus, as well."

"Very good, sir."

Ezra heard the clacking of keys for a moment, and then Robert added, "I can have you on the next flight at five out of Manchester-Boston Regional Airport if that works for you."

"It most certainly does," Ezra answered. "Thank you. Have the car here in half an hour. I'll have my overnight bag, so there'll be no need to check anything in."

"Understood, sir."

Ezra ended the call and stripped off his clothes as he made his way to the bathroom. A quick shower and a bite to eat would be all he needed for the ride to the airport.

CHAPTER 43

SETTLING SOME BUSINESS

Three days after the attack, Stan sat in the parlor.

He had cleaned the room, hired the men to repair the damages, and paid for the broken windows.

What he couldn't do was make Adam better.

Adam was in the ICU in Nashua. Oddly enough, he was in the same room Kenny had occupied.

Stan would ensure all the bills were paid, and Marilyn kept a steady vigil with the young man. If she wasn't at home cleaning, she was at the hospital.

Stan could not do the same. Sitting for even a short time gnawed at the barriers he had built against his violence.

There were two people responsible for Adam's injuries, and Stan needed to settle the score with both. One was Ezra Pettigrew, and he would need to search and find where that man hid. Pettigrew would suffer for the pain he had inflicted on Stan's friends and for the death of Kenny.

Which brought Stan to the other party responsible.

The ghost of the burnt man, as Marilyn had described him.

The burnt man had vanished almost immediately after he had beaten Adam down. Two other ghosts, that of a woman and a large blonde man, had disappeared only a minute or so later. Marilyn's description of the event told Stan that the burnt man was attached to the button, for that had gone right into the lead-lined box. The other two ghosts had lasted until the car was out of range.

Stan finished his tea, which had gone cold, and then left the parlor and then the house. He walked to the barn and retrieved salt, a bottle of lighter fluid and a box of kitchen matches. He slipped them into various pockets as he exited the barn.

In silence, he followed a slim trail that led deep into the woods behind Marilyn's home. He walked for almost an hour, his mind focused on the place where he wanted to be, and before an hour had passed, he was there.

An old cellar hole, half-filled with dirt and ancient bricks, waited for him.

Like Philomena's house, this property, too, belonged to Stan. It had once been owned by his granduncle, and it was a place where Stan had learned to do terrible things to bad people. A place he hated for the violence and pain attached to it.

Failure on his part to perform to his granduncle's expectations had led to swift and brutal punishments.

Stan walked down into the cellar hole, stepping on hard-packed earth, knowing there were bodies buried on either side. He remembered digging their graves while his granduncle had finished off those destined to remain on the property.

At the center of the cellar, Stan squatted and brushed off a circular stone roughly three feet in diameter. When it was sufficiently clean, he retrieved the salt. He poured out a large circle before he placed the lead-lined box in the middle of the circle. At last, he removed the lighter fluid and doused the exterior of the box, and then he opened the container before filling it with fluid.

As he stood and backed away, the burnt man appeared.

The ghost looked around, confused, but when he saw Stan, he tried to step forward, only to find himself trapped.

"Salt?" the dead man sneered.

"Salt," Stan confirmed.

The ghost looked around. "Where the hell are we?"

"Away from my home," Stan stated. "And away from my friends."

The dead man laughed. "Your friends? Was that young kid one of your friends? The one I kicked in the chest a few times?"

"Yes, he is one of them," Stan nodded. "I know this will not stop you, but I do know you are attempting to distract me, to bring my anger to a head."

"It'll work," the dead man grinned.

"No," Stan disagreed. "I cannot be distracted, for what I have planned is already in place. And as for bringing my anger to a head, where do you think it is otherwise?"

The ghost blinked, confused.

"I am forever angry," Stan informed him. "I *am* violence."

"You?" The dead man laughed then shook his head. "You look like you couldn't fight your way outta paper bag, buddy."

"I know."

"If you're violence," the dead man continued, "why don't you let me out of this little ring of salt, and we can fight it out. Show me how tough you are."

"I will not," Stan stated. "I have proven myself to stronger men than you. More importantly, I have proven it to myself. And besides, I have no desire for you to have any sort of satisfaction. You are going to burn, and I am going to watch."

"I can't burn, I'm already dead." Beneath the bravado of the dead man's tone, Stan heard the fear. The ghost had died by fire.

"You may not burn," Stan conceded. "But your button can. I do not know if you will feel the heat as the fire devours it. I doubt it will be pleasant either way. I do not know if there is a hell or a heaven, nor do I care. I will watch the fire. I will enjoy it. Do you understand?"

Fear and true understanding filled the dead man's charred features.

With a shout of rage, the ghost threw himself against the unseen barrier formed by the salt.

The stone shook, and the lead-lined box jumped, splashing lighter fluid around.

For several minutes, Stan allowed the scene to continue, and then he stepped forward, taking the box of matches out of his pocket.

The dead man shrieked, his words nonsensical as Stan struck a match, held the flaming head up for the ghost to see, and then tossed it to where the lead-lined box sat.

Fire erupted from the ground, and Stan retreated.

He watched as the dead man writhed in the center of the salt, which quickly burned away, but there was no escape for the ghost. Whether the dead man felt the pain of the flames or not didn't matter.

The ghost was burning.

Blue flames punched through the dead man's body, and when they finally blazed out of his eyes and mouth, the button exploded.

The earth shuddered and sent Stan stumbling back, dropping him to one knee and leaving him gasping for breath.

When he looked up, the dead man was gone, and a small fire remained. Smoldering bits of the lead-lined box lay against the cellar's walls. For a moment, Stan stood and watched. Then, in silence, he walked to each piece and ground it into the dirt.

Stan did not know how to find information on Ezra Pettigrew, and Pettigrew needed to be punished.

Sitting in the parlor, with the landline beside him on a side table, Stan picked up his small notebook. He flipped through the pages, found the number he needed and dialed it

The phone rang on the other end, and a machine picked up. Once it finished telling him the prompt, Stan spoke into the phone.

"This is Stanley Owens. I am in need of information, and you offered assistance at the cemetery. I am hopeful that this offer still stands. If it does, could you please return this call?"

Stan left the number to Marilyn's house, repeated it, and then hung up the phone.

He put the notebook away and settled into the chair.

With any luck, Shane Ryan would return his call soon, and Stan could hunt Pettigrew down.

And Pettigrew's death, Stan promised himself as he closed his eyes, would not be easy.

⁕

Check out these best-selling series from our talented authors:

GHOST STORIES

RON RIPLEY
BERKLEY STREET SERIES
MOVING IN SERIES
HAUNTED COLLECTION SERIES
DEATH HUNTER SERIES

IAN FORTEY
JIGSAW OF SOULS SERIES
CULT OF THE ENDLESS NIGHT SERIES

SUPERNATURAL SUSPENSE

A. I. NASSER
SLAUGHTER SERIES
SIN SERIES

DAVID LONGHORN
NIGHTMARE SERIES
ASYLUM SERIES

SARA CLANCY
THE BELL WITCH SERIES
BANSHEE SERIES

For a complete list of our new releases and best-selling horror books, visit ScareStreet.com or scan the QR code below!

www.ingramcontent.com/pod-product-compliance
Lightning Source LLC
Chambersburg PA
CBHW050341030726
47503CB00008B/2564